Undertow

Also by Gael Elton Mayo

Honeymoon in Hell
The Devil and the Fool
Nobody's Nothing
Last Seen Near Trafalgar
It's Locked in with You
The Mad Mosaic
A Man in a Panther Skin
The End of a Dream

Undertow

Gael Elton Mayo

Quartet Books
London New York

First published by Quartet Books Limited 1989
A member of the Namara Group
27/29 Goodge Street
London W1P 1FD

British Library Cataloguing in Publication Data
Mayo, Gael Elton
Undertow.
I. Title
823′.914 [F]

ISBN 0 7043 2724 4

Typeset by AKM Associates (UK) Ltd, Southall, London
Printed and bound in Great Britain by
BPCC Hazell Books Ltd
Member of BPCC Ltd
Aylesbury, Bucks, England

My thanks to Governor Jack Shulman of the Rochester Borstal for my visits there in 1986, and to Louis Blom-Cooper QC for the initial arrangement

One

Yesterday I went back to Wissingley after ten years, which is about half my life. Leaving it was the Divide, like crossing a frontier: I have turned to it ever since, whenever I'm cornered, to retire to another land.

Until I was eight we used to swim at night in the peaty black pond with bats darting and jasmine smelling so strong it made us giddy; white roses leaning over us phosphorescent, our naked bodies greenish in the moonlight. Sometimes we went down the narrow path through the cleft in the hill that led to the ocean, frightening at dark. I held her warm hand and was safe. Her hand was small but strong.

They let me out from the borstal on my eighteenth birthday and I stood on the pavement in London and I was nobody. I wondered where to go. They told me she had left home, which I already knew. I don't know where she might be, she never wrote all the time I was Inside. I dare not go to our old place because of the ghosts – and suppose they somehow renewed the lease after all, and she has not gone? I want to see her, but am afraid. Why did she never visit me? The permanent thing, the only thing you can count on, does it short circuit, like the telephone wires at Wissingley in a storm or when a hawk hit them? But that was reparable. If this is final I don't want to know. There was a life she made me believe in, but perhaps it was not true . . . just her delusion, my hallucination . . .

I have a small hope, a scarred limp thing inside me, but familiar, and I do not want to lose it. Finding out might kill it, like the things I discovered when we moved to town, things I wish I had never learned.

So I stood Outside – free – and I thought: Wissingley.

A bus passed with a smell of foul exhaust. I never got used to the city grime and the fumes. I thought of the wild geese with their long stretched necks, arriving out of the sky each spring from some far continent to nest by the pond – and their whooshing take-off from the water into smooth flight, up and away. The city bus was tied to the dog-piss cement, belching lead-smoke, bent on monotonous destination, filled with men removed from their source. At Wissingley every creature was free, choosing its own beat, bedding in ferns and mosses – not dazed in a bus, door to door, office to bed-sitter to grave.

I have done my time and have been let out, I stand on an asphalt street with a cake of prison soap in my pocket. A kid from the Youth Custody Centre with a chip on both shoulders, an identification number but no name. But my possession: a grey smoke of hope like that soggy October smouldering of wet hay. We kept good hay for the ponies but burned the thistles and weeds that Gregg scythed for us; there is a trick in making it burn in damp weather, a countryman's knowledge. I remember, I hold it and am drawn. Wissingley, I want you to be the truth, to please efface all that happened.

Suddenly the damp thistle-smoke flames into fire, not thick yellow-grey, bright orange. Yet also fear. Which is worse? Wissingley is safer than seeing her. I can go to earth there, I can sleep in one of those hollows where deer have lain, like I used to long for in my cell.

There is a strange, slanting shine because it is November now and the sun is low, making horizontal lines like combs across the fields, each tree-shadow sharp and final. The leaves have definite edges outlined in the clear Atlantic light; the yew hedge has grown to a forest, its opening like two black towers, a gateway pointing like arrows across the scraggy meadow that was once the lawn, pointing at nothing, because *the house has gone*.

Yet it is Wissingley. Though the tall trees have been cut down, there is still the same medlar she never liked and the magnolia she loved, grown over with ropes of bindweed and nettles. I tear them off the magnolia in fury; they are brown and weak with autumn and come loose – but the tree is a choked wreck. The same curve in the drive that hid the house until the last moment when it suddenly appeared –

void now because the house where we lived the only important part of our life has gone. Three-hundred-year-old stone. Bulldozed? *So that was why she never would discuss it*. The red dogwood that was only a bush towers like a tree above old levelled stones of a ruin – ruined on purpose, how else? What caused it? The dogwood has lost almost all its leaves and they glow like blood on the grey rocks of the ground – the corpse of a house.

One day my father came to call. I had never seen him before; a stranger not welcome. Looking back, he may have been the first werewolf. Hot, angry talk in the kitchen, chairs scraped, me closed outside in the hall, clammy, scared, *what was happening*? never closed out before. *She* had included me in everything until then, so it must be because of him. A mark on the flagstone floor I saw later, like a scar after he left.

Next day we packed. Also it started to rain and my mother jumped at the first plonking, isolated drops on to the rhubarb leaves outside the kitchen, and she said, 'Who's there? It's footsteps, it's him returning.' And looked at me like a trapped hare with the rain gathering now into a drone.

So then I knew it was his doing we had to leave; she had panic-eyes. When you are eight you feel. You don't think yet in the muddled grown-up way. It is later when you try to reason that the confusion starts. This was clear: we were about to lose something for ever. I knew it, she only suspected with foreboding, yet there was nothing I could do. It's raindrops, not steps, but it's bad. It's the Devil out there in the rhubarb. I wanted to clutch her like a man and say: Don't. But don't what? I was small and eight and did not know what she was doing. Except that we had packed bags and that she should have refused – and that she, who talked to me and told me everything, had not done so this time for the first time. She hadn't told. So neither would she listen. This thing was too big, and I was too small, so she thought. She had signed papers, made arrangements over my head though I was the man of the family and it also concerned me. I knew she was afraid, and I had never known her frightened before. It was her head too, we would both go under.

So he sold Wissingley, I discovered in November ten years later, and maybe the new owner pulled the house down – couldn't be bothered to do what we used to do, patching it up and painting mildew with Granger's Solution and loving its rotten old walls. She knew how to cement leaks and rub down the ponies and treat their sores like a vet – and then come indoors and write her music and cook us rabbit pie. She was a good shot and she killed the rabbits because they ate the vegetables, otherwise she didn't like killing. She planted the vegetables out in spring, in straight lines with a spool of thread. But I suppose the house was derelict really, only I never noticed because I was bewitched.

Night before we left she said, 'Are you glad, Timothy, to be warm in here and not out in dank fox's hole with the roots coming through the ceiling like a grave?'

'Well why would we be *there*?' I asked, astonished with creeping skin.

'We might do worse,' she said.

'But you like the fox,' I said puzzled, 'he's our nearest neighbour, we've left goose bones on his earth every Christmas, on his scraped-out front doorstep under the oak . . .' Anyway she never called me Timothy, just Timmy or old Tim. The name Timothy felt dire and formal.

'Yes, I like him but he smells and I don't like his house. So remember this one,' she said. 'Keep this inside because it has gone. We may be cold, darling, I can't promise.'

Then it was quiet, except for the old clock that ticked out in the hall like it always did so I could not believe any of this was not as sure as the summer pudding or quince jam she made, except that a little draught came in a new way under the kitchen door like a claw. There was her face, she looked at me with light shining out of her eyes. It was then I lost her, but didn't know it.

Day after that she made a pile of photographs and letters and pressed flowers and burned them in the orchard. I watched, cold as stone.

She said, 'You wouldn't want them, Timmy, you never knew the people.'

'Were they my relations?'

'No.'

So she had had secrets all this time. Other people. I knew the ones here, Farmer Gregg and Professor Keating and Ashley and my school. I thought that everything had started here, the past was the present.

'But the furniture Mama?'

'It wasn't ours. This was your father's family place.'

'Haven't you got anything?'

'I've got you,' she said, and I could hear the breakers crashing and rasping up the beach below the hill . . . the undertow at outgoing tide could pull you away. The beach was half a mile beyond, and to hear the waves meant a storm. I stood and stared at the yellow apples that were lying all over the ground. What she was really saying was that everything I had ever known would be gone for ever.

Next day we walked down the drive carrying her big suitcase that weighed a ton as if it must be full of stones. (I found later that it was books.) She collected blue flints. Travel light, she said, burning the light things like photographs and then travelling heavy. Yet there was only one suitcase and a few bags after all those years of life.

I said, 'I thought it was our place,' and she stopped and looked at me square and said, 'It was ours, truly ours. But it isn't now. You can't own a place or a person fully, remember that.' *How* I was to remember.

She touched some of the leaves and smelled them, chewing and spitting out – put her hand into the earth round the moss rose and looked at the dirt on her fingers, and she cried as if she had cut herself. For years she had cherished this rose, calling it her cabbage rose, *spinosissima*, *muscoso* (which I thought were endearments), and was always digging out any surrounding hogweed by its piggish roots. It was her familiar. I started to hate then, but did not know what I was hating.

Farmer Gregg was waiting in his old car at the end of the drive. He opened the door.

'So you wanted to walk it for the last time,' he said, 'like walking the plank . . .'

She didn't answer. He looked down at her the way he had looked at our animals when he fetched them the day before. I sat in the back and stared at their two heads, his red hair and freckled nape – her head dark and today her hair all brushed and tidy, she had pinned it up. She was someone else. I was terrified. Usually they talked – they were completely silent. I did hope he would please, please look after my cat.

It was foggy, the sort of close fog that encircles like the walls of a room. It felt untrue, Farmer Gregg so permanent, so huge and strong, but not strong enough after all to hold us safe inside his tree trunk. The yellow poplar leaves and red hydrangeas glowed in my head like a fire – I was clamped inside myself and no one heard my shriek because it couldn't come out.

At the station he said, 'Let me know . . .' But she never did.

Two

We lived in London. She had a job and I saw little of her. Before – we had talked. Now, we hardly communicated. We had used to gallop the ponies and work at the vegetable garden, in the evenings we read plays or poetry which she explained to me; she would play the piano and sometimes we would sing. She was mine, or rather the world was ours, it started immediately outside the house and I discovered it each day with excitement, no day in any season, any year, was alike. But what lay outside the front door now? A smouldering despair. First, the smell. Thick air and frying oil. Faces of clever people, superior. (I write this looking back, now I am tall, but then I was small for my age which made everything worse.) Sometimes kind people would call me dearie, this was ghastly, my chin trembled trying not to cry and I felt a fool. Occasionally there were tramps, quite young, their feet wrapped in old shoes with cloths and string added, asleep on the concrete. And girls . . . elegant and carefree, sure of themselves – and some of them with green hair in spikes like lunatic dolls – they were scary.

I lost my school that I used to go to on my bicycle, down the lane and then the road, seven miles, with Ashley my best friend, skidding on frosty mornings, full moon still at seven o'clock – and I lost my other schoolfriends too. I went down the street now to a grimy building where screams and sneers echoed in a leafless courtyard of yellowish blackened bricks and everyone was rough and envious. Specially envious, they had it in for each other. They said I talked like the other people, whoever the other people were; they beat me up a few times because of my voice. I couldn't help my voice and didn't like theirs any better. They called me shitface and I answered redshank, which was a bird I liked less than most – it is noisy and restless like the boys in city school – or I called them animals, you weasel, you smell like a badger – and so they gaped . . . What the shit was a redshank, let's see if he's got red balls, let's take his trousers off. And the mob lined up and kicked my crotch. A teacher called them off but my shame remained, it was not for the pain that I cried, but the discovery of the new world – it came out like a stream gushing.

My cat at Wissingley had brown fur, rather thick like mink; he was a Burmese we had found in a ditch, he had been run over but he recovered. The vet said he must be about five – he was grown when we got him; we had no near neighbours and we thought he must have fallen out of a car – he understood everything, he knew he was ours. I wished and longed for him now.

I had not heard the language of these boys before but I soon picked it up and gave back worse because I invented my own; they all used the same words, they invented nothing. New, hideous words came to me, but without pleasure. It was mean, and what was worse, it was *dull*. Wherever I looked was flat and grey. Rat-vomit glue-sniffers. They despised me because I didn't sniff. Why should I get high on something that stank? I stopped wanting to learn and dreamed through the lessons thinking of how when we used to swim in our pond our skin looked the colour of iodine because of the peat and leaves on the bottom, yet the water was clear. Galloping my pony in the great wind that smelled of juniper instead of their rancid sweaty armpits and stinking shoes. The classrooms had naked lightbulbs hanging down like targets for beginners with air guns. After a while there was a great achievement: the boys ignored me.

But I lost Farmer Gregg's ploughed field with the white gulls all over it like a crop. I lost my mother who had also been my friend, I grew cagey with her, I don't know what caused it, she wasn't Mama any more, she was Ma or Mum or just 'you'. But she changed too; she had seemed tall and reliable, but now in London she seemed smaller and fragile. We were unsafe. I grew afraid of what might come and maybe held her responsible, I don't know, only that I used to trust her and could not now. She had let this happen.

Then she lost her job. She was at least there when I got home, but dawdling round, absent, hair straggling – not even the photograph of the Wissingley person. She made cakes and took them to the old women who sat in doorways of the dark mansion near my school. She became a self-ordained social worker, everyone's helper, easy to get, giving away her clothes – not that she had many. I didn't feel fair, I was a new mean person and I felt cross with her. Not that I minded old ladies having cakes – they were probably not used to real things, since in London people ate tinned and frozen food I noticed, factory cakes in packages. But charity seemed to me misguided, based on guilt or inventing a duty, and – maybe even useless – because surely it makes it worse to give a tramp a steak, a glimpse of another life, unless he can go on having it all the time? I started to think; when I was nine, ten, eleven I started to try to work things out and see constructively – but I could only ask myself questions, I could not give the answers, and I disliked my own company very much.

'Can I have Jake sent here?'

'He's a country cat, he'd hate the town.'

'Yes. Indeed he would . . . Does he *know* I'll fetch him somehow, sometime?'

'Cats have no sense of time.'

'How do you know?'

'Well of *course*. They haven't got calendars and clocks.'

'I wish I could write to him.'

'I'm sure he's all right.'

'I hate you.'

'I love you Timmy. I can't help what happened.'

I wanted to hug her then, but could not do so.

She found herself odd jobs, like making pizzas for the delicatessen up the street, or lampshades for a gift shop. People came to see us. I don't know where she found them, she made friends. I hated the friends. In the country there had been people we knew, men we did things with, like cutting trees and then having tea; or Gregg who was part of our life, or Christmas in Professor Keating's cottage.

In the city, friends just came and sat. And drank. And held her hand, which angered me. They made a fence between me and my mother, more than a fence, a canyon caused by an earthquake; everything quaked and then settled again, alien. What cataclysm had caused my father to visit us? In the beginning I still dreamed of Wissingley at night and the earth squelching in spring and the birds twittering and gurgling like fizz water, there were so many; then I would wake and think: but that isn't the house creaking – it's Sam creaking my mother's bed in the next room.

I would go downstairs to the basement and make coffee and I would hear the feet. They all went north or east in the morning, I could tell the time by the feet. First the daily women, dragging their bunions in scuffed shoes; then the brisk, assured walk of young men going to get the tube to the city. Then cars. But before all this there was the milkman with his whirring electric van. I liked him. The town has its thing too but I would not admit this at first because it brought us such harm. The milkman was my first good contact though; I was the one who put the bottles out at night with the note: 'Two milk, one butter. Hope you like your job.' He used to wave to me in the street when I saw him later and it gave me a good feeling, his wave.

*

We lived above a grocer's shop. Our street was like Basin Street in her old jazz records, where all and any folk meet, sooner or later everyone goes down that street, it must lead somewhere, but not for us.

But people. I could hardly believe it. Someone called Erskine she hadn't seen since Chicago. Chicago? I never knew she'd even been there. Then I discovered she had had a whole other life before I was born. Well of course she had, only why did she never talk of it? It had been as if her first memories started at Wissingley with me, we were both born there. And now: Fred and Jim and oh why hello Mr Bradford. She had been an actress once. So where was I? A non-person. Not even an idea.

Fred looked at me in the street, and I was a non-person longing to become someone, to be liked, to fit in, but he was not too interested; he looked back at her, dismissing me, so it felt as if I was not really there. I started to dread whoever it was we would meet next: did you know her too? How well? Like they were taking her away.

One of them said, 'Whose son is he then?' and I flung out and socked his jaw. 'My father's of course!' I shouted. 'Didn't you know she was married?' And in that moment I thought: maybe she wasn't married. Also I wished I was not 'his' son, since he did us down. And there stood this man swaying but not really cross, because I was still small, unfortunately they did not know how big I was inside; my mother was excusing me by saying they were rough at school and the man actually looked amused (it was a *joke*) which was the kill, because the worst thing is to be laughed at. He just rubbed his chin and looked back at his real concern, which was my mother. He reminded me of Gregg's Alsatian who was always trying to get Jake. So where were my mother's claws?

I ran off down the street and wished I could hug Jake and bite the fur behind his neck. He used to fight the Alsatian back. He would catch squirrels and rats and be fierce and then come in and let me wrestle with him and only have paddy paws. I wondered if our animals came sniffing round the house wondering where we were or if they knew they belonged to Gregg. Oh for Gregg to come and kick Fred and Jim and Erskine and Mr Bradford. Gregg was a proper man, he coped. He looked beautiful with his red hair, tall as a copper beech with the sky in his eyes, to count on certain sure. He took us shopping once a week because we didn't have a car. We got supplies like flour and sugar and wine and then went to the pub where they let me in too. That was a real little town, a place you could get to know . . . In July there was a fair . . . But what's the use? Bury it. Yet it would not lie down and die, it was my ghost, I saw it everywhere, it followed me and I couldn't get it off my back.

As well as Jake we had a dog. He was such a dud we called him Duddo, but I liked him. He was another stray who had just decided to live with us; he fawned too much and the one time a prowler came he licked his hand. But he had golden eyes and was grateful, he understood we had given him a home. I wondered whether Gregg's dogs fought the poor old fellow. We had always wanted a huge, splendid dog – lucky now we never got one to be left behind.

Before Gregg scythed the grass in high summer it grew very tall – when I was small I used to hide in it.

Instead of birds in trees there were green lace-wings and red and black devil bugs and grasshoppers – the thicker stems were sometimes twined round with convolvulus – it was another world where buttercups made a yellow light.

My mother liked taming fierce things, which was why Gregg let her ride his stallion, also no one else could get near him. He was called Nero and Gregg used him for breeding; he liked mother to exercise him, otherwise he would go wild. He panicked in thunderstorms. He was beautiful and dangerous but my mother had a way of speaking to him in a special voice and soothing him, they had some sort of kinship; he would allow her to walk him and not gallop till she gave the order, then they would be off and away across the skyline in a streak together, her black hair and his black mane flying . . .

When I got home I sat down with my eyes closed to concentrate on not caring, after being laughed at by the man I had hit. (We had two Welsh ponies because of me, so that we could ride together – but Ma was a real rider. I said once, 'Let's have a hawk,' only she said, 'You have to find a fallen one. You can't just order hawks.')

And now she was in the street talking to a fallen rook or some common starling. And Jake, the real fur person, was left to hiss at the farm dogs, and Nero to pound the turf hundreds of miles away.

'Dear Milkman, please leave some poison too. There's someone I hate.'

He didn't wave that day. 'Dear Milkman, I'm sorry. Please don't let me lose your friendship. I am lonely. Two milk, two butter, six eggs. I hope you have a family. She forgot my birthday.'

He waved later but looked embarrassed.

A week afterwards I found a card in my room with a woollen scarf. The card said, 'Dearest Timmy, this isn't much, we are broke. Happy birthday all the same.' So she had not forgotten. Only I had not found it on the day probably because my room was in such a mess. I tried to thank her, but it didn't come out properly. Besides, why hadn't she made me a cake? I gave the scarf to the milkman. He was amazed. 'Cashmere?' he said, and I saw that its dark colours were beautiful. I would have liked it back, but it was too late. I felt all crooked and crazy inside.

Then I met Swan at school.

Three

He was called Swan because his name was in Hindi or some unknown language that no one even tried to pronounce. He had been there all along but I had not noticed him at first – he kept apart and was quiet and detached. The others left him alone because he was different, and also with a certain respect because he was taller and older than any of us – he was only in the same class because he did not work or try to work, and so was behind in his studies. Yet he was clever. I didn't work either because I was bored and had anyway learnt far more already with my mother at Wissingley.

After school Swan never went home. He said there were ten in one room and they never noticed if he was there or not, just had more space without him. He used to rummage and pick up junk, clean it and sell it, and he made money. He said he planned to get on. I started a new life with him with my new person. The other person inside was cross because it remembered Ashley and was ashamed of selling junk. But so what? How are you Ashley, are you well? I am disgusted but getting used to it, a question of habit. Ashley was an orphan who lived with Professor Keating, he was determined to get a scholarship for university.

Swan had a blind spot; he followed his road like a horse with blinkers. Though he was clever, he was not interested in real things. What were they? he asked. Well, my butterfly collection or my mother's blue flints, agates and yellow quartz. He laughed and laughed and said he was thirteen. My mother had a friend called James, I told him, who thought these things were interesting, and he was forty, or anyway old. (He was a new friend of hers, the first one I liked.) But I respected Swan, he mastered and shaped his life. Maybe his belief was more real than my butterflies. I marvelled at them, yet to him they were dust. He chose what he did (unlike me) and was ruthless and content. He didn't expect, he didn't question, he existed and planned. That's the way it is, he would say, so use what you've got, and he would shrug. I admired him, but he made my butterflies foolish, so I put them away under the bed in the big cracked box with the glass top. I couldn't quite make myself throw them away, but I hid them and tried to forget where.

'How old was I when we first went to Wissingley, Ma?'

'Three,' she said.

'Did you regret it?' She had given up her Freds for it, hadn't she, as I had now discovered . . .

'*Regret*?' She stared at me. We were on proper speaking terms again. But she seemed shaken by the question. 'Regret?' she said, 'Regret what? Old Tim, was I ever glad not to sleep in *his* nettlebed again.'

She spoke as if I were fifty and knew what it was all about. Except for what she withheld – I mean she answered direct questions as if I knew the context.

'Was that all? Getting out of a bed?'

'Of course not. What's got into you? It was miraculous to be at Wissingley.'

'You don't seem to miss it now.'

'It was perfect. Perhaps that is why it could not last, too perfect.'

That made me cross. Why should something not be perfect? It was lasting for all those other people who were still living round there. Why must we accept?

She was murmuring something about London being instructive, and I felt a rage welling up inside me that I could not get out.

'One day, I would like to talk with my father,' I said.

'He lives abroad, I haven't got his address.'

It was a dissolving sand-pattern when the sea washes over it. Everyone else knew their father's address, why were we so different? Even Ashley, who had no parents, knew who they had been. His father was a scientist who died, Professor Keating was a distant relative, so it was in order.

'Suppose we needed something, could we find him?'

'Need?' She laughed then, with her rather small, white teeth reminding me of a vixen. She laughed at our problems and Swan laughed and I didn't see the point. 'Is my father not interested in me at all . . . if I am his son?'

She hugged me then. 'Oh Timmy, I am sorry. But why pretend?'

So that was how it was. Why pretend? And she did not want to speak of him. I had longed to be hugged again in all this time, but suddenly in her warm smell and soft skin and with her long hair hanging on me, I didn't want it any more. Not pity, not consolation, maybe not even her. I was a man, Swan's friend. I pushed her away, feeling strangely embarrassed.

At the time of this conversation we were in the bathroom, we had been hanging new curtains which she had made, then stood staring out at the view which was the best in the house, it looked on to the back garden. Now she started brushing her hair with her arm raised. Miraculous then, was it, Wissingley, at least you haven't forgotten it like I had thought - and I noticed how white her arm was underneath near the armpit with a little blue vein showing. The vein upset me. I thought: she is vulnerable, the vein could be cut. *They* are not vulnerable, the other people. Their fathers or brothers or husbands would come. It isn't safe any more for us. Gregg isn't here. We knew safe people, but they are gone. We have no man in the family except me, and she won't admit that. She is making a deal here, not seeing that the people she meets in the street will bring danger, she is mistaking jackals for dogs, and there is trouble coming.

'Why do we stay here?' I asked.

'It's easier to get work in a city.'

So at last it snapped. I accepted. I left her alone and went out more and more to find Swan. We had lost

Wissingley hadn't we? So stop floundering about in an afterlife.

I started to notice what she was making of it here: two rooms above a grocer but we also had a garden out at the back because the grocer said we could use it, he only needed one end for his crates. There was an outside staircase with a plexiglass roof like a fire escape (it leaked when it rained), and this joined our rooms to the basement without going through the shop, though we had a tiny hall where the door opened on to the front steps, and another rickety staircase led below. The basement was ours too, it was the room where we lived most in the daytime, the kitchen was next to it and there was an old piano. Lucky about the piano, she still played and in rare good moments, until my voice broke, we sang duets. There was a hob grate where she burnt logs, and a hearthstone made of a wide piece of dark-green slate.

We were on feet level for breakfast. Below feet level – we saw out of the window up to their knees. We could also see the postman or whoever was at the front door. I knew about the people by their shoes, and by the way they walked, whether they were beaten down, had given up, or still believed in the big chance. I made a study of feet and knew whether they were cowards or brave, whether they walked proudly or timidly, whether they knew what they wanted, or were undecided, and I became a fetishist about shoes; shoes are very important, a good suit with bad shoes is a dead loss. I hated my own shoes. When I made money with Swan I planned to buy new ones, also for *her*. But it's amazing the price of good shoes.

The garden: she grew white violets and a clematis that had large, very pale blooms like moon flowers, I mean the old dream moon, not the modern one they have trampled and made solid. She grew a bush with pink buds and a lace-cap ring of star flowers round its centre in a circle, so we had moons and stars outside. At the end of the garden there was an ancient apple tree that sometimes produced a few apples, russet and sharp-tasting.

'We've got a patch of earth still Timmy,' she would say. 'We're lucky – lots of people have no earth.' And she would fork the soil that gave out the smell of the land that lies under London. 'Hear the blackbird rustling in that bush,' and I observed her and wondered, could she *really think* we were lucky? Next-door garden had a fig tree and it leaned over our fence with smooth grey arms. We had a bench and sat under the branches on summer nights drinking wine. When it rained we went up the outside stair to bed in our raincoats, it was shorter than going down into the basement and up the rickety staircase in front.

'Are we lucky?'

'Why mope?' she said, 'I like it here, the grocer gives credit, and free leftovers, let's make it all right. Take your black glasses off and see the light. I like the pubs and the life, it's exciting.'

'I'm not allowed into the pubs.'

'Don't be a drag, old Tim.'

She was right, I was a nagger and a drag, but I didn't mean to be. It's what you make of it; she was trying.

'Lucky there's a piano,' I said, trying.

'I knew there was when I accepted the house. So if we get really broke, as a last resort, I can give piano lessons.'

'You call this a house? It's a rabbit hutch with ladder stairs everywhere instead of burrows.' It was no use, I was cross again because I knew she hated teaching piano. She liked composing, playing - and what had happened to the music she didn't write any more? And if she didn't think we were already broke, then what did she call it? *Anyone* would be cross. Also - it was only one aspect - certainly she was making this side of our life all right - but there was something else that gave me the creeps, it was the visitors. They brought undercurrents. In Wissingley I used to run to open the door if the bell rang - it was rare anyway to have callers and an adventure - even when it was Gregg sometimes come to fetch my mother to cope with his wife. Because Gregg's wife had fits. She shivered and saw scorpions and spotted men. The only person who could settle her cool and quiet was Ma, who would croon her songs with old, forlorn tunes, or give the creature a bran bath; the woman was like a thin, old grasshopper that had got out of chirp. Strange wife for a big, burly man like Gregg, I used to think. But the doorbell . . . it could be Ashley, or the postman . . . it was worth answering, a surprise, something that mattered.

In London I hated it. 'Oh hello Tim,' they would say, and look beyond and over my shoulder. 'How's the homework?' In other words: get lost. They wanted me out. Specially Fred (the one I had hit). So I would hang around and ask questions and be a nuisance. But fortunately, I too had my other world of Swan.

I watched the new thing Swan was doing: he was selling potted plants door to door for double the price he had bought them for. He rang doorbells and said it was for the blind people. Blind was right, it was a blind if the housewives didn't see through him. He was lucky because they looked *at* him. He was wonderful to look at, long and slim with gentle eyes and blue-black hair like a cormorant's neck feathers. And careful on these occasions to be clean and neatly dressed. So they looked at him in surprise, then down at the dear little green plants in the pots.

'What a nice boy to help the blind,' they would say, never thinking to ask for his credentials.

Then, 'What green fools,' he would say to me, and we would go off together and have a drink. (Nettles are green. Nettlebed. My parents must have been married or it would not have been such a big thing to get out of his bed, she wouldn't have switched off so entirely and refuse to speak about him. I have noticed that with marriage people feel stuck. A lover can just get out of bed and leave. I read a lot about this in the *Evening Standard* the grocer gave me, after he had finished with it.) Swan was wary of trying to be in a pub, as he was under age, but he was tall and looked mature so he managed to get away with dashing in and saying, 'Can I have a bottle to take out please? It's Mum's birthday,' and it didn't occur to them that maybe he was under eighteen until after he had gone.

He never used the same pub twice. I liked the way he drank – it was more fun than glue.

When he drank he schemed. Bigger things. One had to get on. 'This is my first capital,' he said after the plants, 'so we won't drink it all. I invested my junk money in this ivy and aspidistra crap. It is small, but it's a principle, invest and resell. It will end up big. I'm looking for the next thing, the better one. Why don't you have any ideas?'

I didn't answer, I was struck by the fact that I had not got one single idea. I was basking in his sunshine-moonshine. I didn't doubt he would end up big, as he said, he was already big to me: glamorous, successful, fascinating. Also he knew girls. He was worldly. I did not make any other friends at school, there was no need. Swan opened up such a view I was hypnotized – anyway the other boys were louts. I didn't even like their harmless pot and they thought I was sissy; maybe I was – the one time I tried, and started taking off, it was uneasy, it was not pleasure – whereas alcohol excited me and made me believe anything could happen. Swan did not care either way. All things were alike to him, he would try anything, take or leave – and when he was with me he drank. He would never attempt to make a person different from what they were. At the time I thought this great, he did not tease or tell a person what to do, though he could be disparaging. Later I realized it was because he didn't care. He seemed to me like a man of thirty. The boys at school would fight, torture each other, have nose bleeds, smell of dirty clothes – and all the time Swan would be cool, smooth as a reed, equally supple – bending with the wind or keeping apart; he was born of a long, dark vanilla bean that had married an eel.

'My father was a nettle,' I said once.

'You talk funny. What's a nettle anyway?'

'Haven't you ever been to the country?'

'Nope.'

'Nettles sting.'

'So your mother got stung.' He laughed.

'What's funny?'

'Maybe she liked it. Stings feel good.'

I lost him sometimes as if he spoke another language. 'Little stings, gentle ones,' he said, with his eyes in dreamy slits.

He had entered his world of experience where he was a man and I was still undersized. Physical sensations he knew about, that I wanted perhaps but hadn't had. I was proud of being his friend, and I knew that through him I would learn many things.

Four

My mother gave piano lessons, which is what I had dreaded though knew would come to pass. It tired her and made her feel drained, she said, it was not her vocation to teach. Something inside her was beginning to die, though I could not say I had foreseen it. The whole world was dying, anyway, cold summers and blight, over-population, cut-down forests. A bird starts dying the day it is in a cage, I had read somewhere. It eats and drinks and sings but the spirit has gone, people do not realize that a bird sings out of loneliness, or to protect its nest. I had no cure to offer, except one new thing, I brought her whisky.

'Where did you get it?' she asked at first.

'Swan's father keeps a pub,' I lied. Lies are habit, only the first one counts.

She spent a lot of time cooking and preparing beautiful meals for the visitors who came at night. There were strange new foods we had never had at Wissingley, like bamboo shoots and coriander leaves; the table was exotic. But she did not read and did not write music any more. Why did these people always come to us? Could they not invite her out sometimes?

They ate the dinner she made with relish. They started to eat her. She was a giver. Before – it used to be the moors outside and the curlews sounding ethereal and making our supper feel safe indoors. Now there were her lovers, I was the other person in the rooming house. I suppose I could have dined with them, but I preferred to eat the remains next day, delicious cold for breakfast.

They all seemed like lovers. Looking back I think there were two, though they were all potentials. James was the first, and the only one I liked, for whom I wanted to be acceptable, not a brat. He cleared the horde also, his presence took charge and gradually the crowd who were draped like scarves all over the furniture, lolling on the sofa when I came home from school, dispersed. James emerged out of these visitors but he was another sort. For a short time he made our life rich. I even had dinner with them because he talked to me too, I started to learn what family life could be like, I started to *like London*. James took me to picture galleries, me, not just Ma. I learned about painting, a new subject. He liked reading aloud (which Swan said was poncey), he was fascinated to learn what I had thought natural, that Ma and I had read Chekhov together since I had been small, on winter afternoons in the country. 'Amazing,' he said. What was amazing? It was dark by four, it was our natural life.

I understood then Ma's pleasure in getting a dinner ready; we would lay the table together and make little bunches of leaves from the garden and discuss what sauce she would make for the fish.

James started me on different things, Rabelais and

John Donne which he said schoolboys liked. I suppose he meant boys like Ashley because at my school they read only comics or sex magazines. I laughed and enjoyed Rabelais, 'rubbing bacons'. Ma preferred Donne, she used to cry sometimes when James read the love poems. Was she remembering some old Erskine? Or the days when she tried to read Joyce to me (it failed, I could not manage to grasp it). Maybe she cried because James had a deep voice and made the love poems disturbing – a person could cry for something they never had. Or did she have a dream man and could it be him? He talked to me as someone who mattered. He brought things, a pheasant and some Beaujolais, or when he was broke, chorizo and Rioja. I asked him what he did, and he told me he wrote travel books; I learned about other countries and started to see England as an island . . . and the world not lost and dying any more, it was not too late to save it, the ecologists were right. I was stirred with new desires, to *do* something about things. But what? Should I join the Greenpeace people? They went about it the wrong way . . . how could they gain more power?

James wore wonderful clothes – thin knitted ties, a tweed jacket, a dark-grey flannel suit – and on Saturdays jeans with a big, thick sweater. He had a coat with a fur collar – and *shoes* . . . I loved his shoes.

Then she met Sam. It was as if the house came loose from its moorings and rocked like a ship; the radar didn't work, we sailed head-on into waves as high as cliffs, force-ten gale but no one heeded the weather report. Somewhere in the wreckage James lost us; I held on to the driftwood. She was busy, she was out, she was someone else who didn't hear.

James came back once, he sat on the sofa beside a pile of books he had come to fetch; there was a strain, I wanted to speak but could find no words, his face looked stern. Ma was quiet, she just stood with her back turned, looking out of the window. I tried to get away and leave them to their business, but the floorboards creaked under my tiptoes and I froze. The silence was a tight wire. Then James got up and left.

I stood in the doorway and watched him go down the street; I was Duddo, who knew the owner was going away and that he was left behind. I wanted to call out, 'James . . . I'll miss you James . . . can't *I* keep seeing you? You are my friend . . . please don't leave me too . . .' but he didn't turn round because he didn't hear my words, they remained inside me. It wasn't my affair, I couldn't beg him back. So he just walked out of our life down that short-cut street of ours, traffic-jam-at-commuter-time street. Short cut to where? I hated our street. *She* had thrown *him* out, but the result was as if he was leaving us.

I glared furiously at my mother. Was she a fool or a bitch? To my surprise she looked frightened and miserable.

'I can't help it Timmy. Not two at once. You'll understand one day,' and she turned her face away, I was dismissed.

James had brought us peace and he took it away with him when he left.

'You never thought *I* might miss him,' I said, before I went out, and when I shut the door chips of old paint fell, showering all over the floor.

There were no more delicious dinners, she didn't eat. She prepared food for me absently, and jumped when the telephone rang, rushing to get there in time. The mail lay unopened. Sam had the opposite effect from James, he made her distraught and somehow used-up. I sang, 'Sam, the dirty old accordion man,' but she paid no heed. She had a secret, closed face, she would smile in some private world where no one else entered, but she grew wan.

Sam was the first fierce thing she did not want to tame. Not a fallen hawk, one that soared, she was the one who fell – then they swooped away together into the sky out of reach, and she turned fierce too.

I asked Swan if he knew any voodoo. He only sniggered and said let her alone to run wild with a fellow, it was good for her. I tried to convince him that I felt it would bring evil, but he only said, 'She is lucky.'

'*Luck*?' I said. 'He will bring bad luck, I know it.'

'You're no bloody fortune-teller. How do you know?' But I did. It was ice on crops in May. Sam usually leaves the house at about three in the morning, I would rather not hear but can't help being awake, I wander round my room and can't settle. She takes pills. It says on the bottle: one at night if required, I've seen them in the bathroom. She must take about three because they have disappeared so fast. She never took sleeping pills before. If their thing is great, as Swan says, why does she need pills? Why does he have to go home, is that why I hear her crying sometimes, because she can't have this thing whole? A person doesn't need a hang-up on their mother to care if she looks like a zombie. Old Ma, my friend, for God's sake . . . this thing is *bad*.

There are his remains all over the place in the morning. He's a vodka drinker; dirty glasses and cigar butts and bits of her clothing all over the room. She used to be neat and tidy. I suppose she starts undressing at dinner. If he wants her all the time, doesn't it make him fond? Doesn't he care if she catches cold going up the outside stair with no clothes on? Or does he keep her warm with the fire from the rockets he shoots . . .? It says in the books that people in love are glowing, but her shine has gone. Caught in a weasel trap, can't move, can't stop it happening . . . Something about it is sick.

'Damn you Swan,' I said, 'you've got to help. The house is on fire.' I mumbled about my grandfather nearly dying of frostbite in Russia and being saved just in time (it was *her* grandfather, she had told me once). He looked at me then in amazement. 'What's got into you?' he said. 'What's anyone's grandfather got to do with this?'

'I don't know, I'm mixed up,' I said. 'Her parents

are dead, we have no family, no one at all except each other. It's not like you, you've got a huge family and don't know what it's like to have none, anyway you don't care for them. She's all I've got. No father. No one else. Don't you understand? Fathers and brothers protect, lovers destroy, anyway this one does. Wouldn't you look after your mother?'

'Don't need to, Father does.'

'Exactly.'

He understood then because it was selfish and he understood selfish things. So though he wasn't keen on 'fooling with Sam', he said that if it meant so much, then all right. He was loyal, in a strange way, we had had a cold friendship before – this was the first thing he would plan that would not be for what he could get out of it himself. Except maybe a kick, he said, at the last moment.

We lay in ambush for Sam for three nights running but it did not work, he found parking space in the street in front of the house and there were too many people. On the fourth night there was no room; he slowed down and turned into the side street which is quiet; we were in luck, there was no one about. All we needed was five minutes. We weren't going to kill him, just mark him up and frighten him, make him not want to come back.

He had the longest car I have ever seen, custom-made I suppose. He got out and locked it very carefully, I saw he was wearing gloves, it looked sinister. Then he turned and started to walk, as sure of himself as if he owned the world. We stood in front of him and barred the way, hands linked, and Swan flicked his knife out. Sam looked astonished to see that it was me, he recognized me, though I had never seen him really close. This spoiled it because he was scornful rather than scared, he grew angry and his face darkened.

Then something terrible happened to *me*: I chickened. I told Swan to stop. I didn't like the knife and hadn't meant real blood, I had only just meant to frighten him. But that was not all: it was that I saw him face to face for the first time and he was beautiful, my mother's beautiful lover. I was seized. I didn't want to spoil the bones of his straight nose, I felt wrong. I felt something I could never explain to Swan: it was that James would not approve, I would be going over to the wrong side.

Swan was furious. 'You yellow squit,' he said, and threw his knife down. It jumped like a stone doing ducks and drakes. He picked it up and walked off. I stared at Sam, who (like everyone else) was much taller than me. He put out a hand and felt my shoulder blades. 'You're thin,' he said. 'I'd better send you a hamper.'

I ran. Scalded with scorn, Sam's scorn, Swan's scorn, and the terror of losing my only friend. I ran after Swan who had reached the corner of the street, I caught up with him and he turned round and faced me. We glared at each other. Then suddenly he burst out laughing. Christ how I loved him for that – because if I had lost Swan I would have lost the world.

'Come on you silly rat,' he said, and we went down the narrow back street to the pub on the corner where he did his trick of going in and getting a bottle and coming right out fast.

We sat on the ground inside a warehouse which was farther away, and started to drink. I tried to make it clear that I had not been frightened, just changed my mind. Swan said, 'Oh you and your Right. You're like some preacher and I'll never listen to you again. It's balls about Right. Who made the rules? Only a bunch of shitsters who take the pickings and use the rules for themselves. Well I make my own rules.'

If I ever had any self-respect, it died then. I admired Swan. A policeman appeared in the street so we moved farther inside the hallway and sat behind a packing case. We got drunk and Swan gave me a lecture. He said we could easily have marked Sam, nothing more, but that kind of man is vain and would not like it, it would have made him stay away. The knife had only been for effect, he did not mean to use it, and would have stuck to the plan of fists. He said he thought Sam was fine and that my mother was lucky, all he regretted was a good fight. I said the knife had been a shock. He said, so what's a knife? and that I was the biggest jerk he had ever met. What did I care who my mother went to bed with? I said it wasn't who, it was how it was affecting her home, but could not explain and got into a muddle. Anyway he did not understand about homes, his own meant nothing to him - ten in one room.

Finally he said, 'You've got to decide which way you're pointing. Lose this bullshit someone brought you up on, it's only made you a mess. You'll never get anywhere with these principles and changing course.'

He must be right . . .

‘And you talk like some schoolteacher, or some shitty grandpa,’ he went on, ‘you don’t sound normal.’

(Did Ashley also talk like me?)

‘Now we’ll go and find some girls,’ he said. It was a let-down. An electric feeling was coming from him that I found exciting. I’d have sooner stayed together than gone after girls. And I didn’t say I’d never had one, it would have been the final end between us. Luckily since we were drunk, I hoped he might not notice how I handled them.

Five

I left school when I was fourteen, but did not tell my mother; she was busy doing what I called wasting her time. It would seem to me that a woman with a rich lover should not need to give piano lessons if she hates it – and get tired. There was a time when I would have liked her pride – now I was conscious of great waste. Living for Sam, scurrying about getting grouse in season . . . She was qualified to look for a decent job. But the idea was to remain free – not tied – always available.

Once I saw two men talking to her outside the front door, I heard the word Chicago – and then one of them offered her a part in a film. Saved at last! . . . But she refused. She said she didn't want to leave town, she had a boy at home at night. That's not all she has at home at night, thought the boy, and slammed the window down hard, so that the sash cord broke. She refused! . . . hadn't even asked what part, what sort of movie – but just the idea of anything taking her away made it out of the question. Besotted indeed . . .

I came and went at the same hours as when I was at school, so it should not be discovered. The reason I left – apart from boredom and the feeling I was not learning anything – was because there had been a riot in my class, they attacked the teacher. I didn't agree and stood up for him – at which point they beat me up too. Then a group called the ILEA wanted to interview me and I refused; though I was against my class and sorry for the teacher who was only doing his best with a bunch of foulmouths, I was not going to go so far as to discuss it with an authority or take sides. There were no sides for me – but in any case it seemed a waste of time to stay on. The only person I liked was Swan, though he often told me I was a fool, but I saw him as the gateway to the future. I did not regret James any more because I knew he would disapprove of everything I was doing.

However, when Swan graduated to stealing, a rift came between us, and though he told me to forget my stupid values, I could not quite manage it. Perhaps this was hypocritical, as I had not minded when he cheated about prices, selling things to housewives – but then the customers seemed to have an option, they did not *have* to buy the goods – stealing was different and I said so. He only shrugged and said, 'So what do I care? You'll come to it in time. What are we supposed to do if everything is beyond our price range?'

We remained companions, I liked his city grit and the strength of his detachment. I don't know what he liked in me – perhaps someone to show off to – but we quarrelled more frequently and I saw less of him. Yet he was my backbone, my need – a useful alibi also, I said I was going to his house when I went out at night (though I had never seen inside his home) and my mother believed it. In her strange way she did care about what I did and liked to know where I was: a piece of furniture that should be in place. A chair is missed in a room if it is removed, even if not specially noticed when it is there. She thought of Swan as 'my friend' – though she had never met him properly – just seen him to wave to in the street.

Swan said, 'You can make money my way. Doesn't your mother need money? That slob with his big car must be loaded, why don't we try him? Even in your values, he must owe your mother something, we would only be taking what is hers.'

'I don't know where he lives,' I said. 'And we would be the first ones he would suspect.' But I was answering not as if it were wrong – just that it might not work. He let it go. But from then on he had insinuated a thought into me: to get her something. Sam coming to dinner in his black snake of a car, saying he would buy her a good piano (I overheard, it was his idea) and then just bringing himself as if it were a gift, and leaving her to take sleeping pills. I never saw any flowers; there was no small, precious object she might cherish.

Swan said, 'Let him be no good. Then she may see through him one day. All the same, it would be a pity – it seems to be high-powered screwing and that is rare.' When he took on his face of superior knowledge – the chemistry of sex – I was Duddo.

He had many girls and some older women of twenty-five, but his main girlfriend was Suzy, who was his own age; she had a sister called Rachel who – at last and overdue – was my first girl. We were in a pub on one of the nights when there is live music and we were let in, they did not actually ask our age. Perhaps we all look old nowadays. There was a man singing into a mike, holding it up close to his face like a lollipop that he might lick – like commercials on the telly that try to make eating sweets look sexy. I did not mean to be against things so often and in some ways it made me feel tragic. But they all drooled over this singer and I thought: he hasn't got a real voice at all – any donkey can bray into a microphone and a sound comes out and fools all the other jackasses who listen . . . he and his lollipop look obscene.

I said so to Rachel and she said I talked like an old man, and why was I so angry? so I looked at her with interest. At least now, I was *old*. Suddenly I wanted to squeeze her – though more as a friend as it turned out – but I was in a hurry. When I kissed her she had a faintly acid smell like hops brewing from a beer factory. But we went home to the place where she lived with Suzy, who had stayed behind, and I managed this thing that is so much talked about, but with our clothes on, awkward and giggling, both trying to pretend we were old hands and experienced. It was disappointing. I suggested we have a bath together, I had noticed there was a beautiful bathroom and hoped it might be sexy, but afterwards she still retained her special, rather cloying smell. Maybe she was just not for me. Was this all there was to it – was this fumbling arrangement the great thing all the fuss was about? So what of Heathcliff and all those romantic novels? Who could I discuss such an important question with . . .? Not Swan – he had a block whenever I mentioned books and would grow quite angry.

Swan remained our group leader, a sort of hero. Whereas in school he was detached and apart, the girls and hangers-on in the outside world were another matter. And for me – there was Rachel, so I had a girl now and was like the others. She grew on me as a friend, a kind companion, possibly she had been lonely before and it was a mutual compromise; I even became accustomed to and grew to quite like her weird smell – but she said I was under-sexed. I thought: it's that there aren't any coloured lights. It's like satisfying hunger with a cheese sandwich, which I would anyway prefer toasted. Or maybe it was true that I was under-sexed; I had no high opinion of what we did together, except that apparently it made me a man – and she did become a need – however disappointing it was not to be able to talk, for, like Swan, she did not read. I was sorry for her, because when I left her to go home she always cried . . . and these would be the times, after I got back to my own bed, when Wissingley would still come rushing back to me like a fever and I would ache for it in all my bones far more than I wanted any girl. I would smell the gorse-scrub and hear the birds singing at day-break and remember getting up in the first light and running, belting down to the beach . . . And how Ma taught me as a small boy to swim and dive through the huge waves that were so frightening, rising up like jaws above us, the spume like hoary breath coming out, ready to clamp down – so I would scream, overwhelmed in terror, but she made me plunge head-first right through them and learn not to fear. Once when I was seven a wave got me sideways and I was battered with the stones it contained and thrown up on to the shore, stunned and rolled over and over. She picked me up and rocked me in her arms and laughed with all the water streaming out of her long, black hair, strangling like seaweed round my neck. I felt tiny and afraid – if this was Nature then I hated the sea. But I learned to dive.

And now when the Wissingley fever got me I would remember those times on the beach and somehow I connected it with sex – this was the feeling I had expected – something huge and overpowering – I had been tricked.

Like all fevers, it would pass. Afterwards the person has either died or recovered. So I would try another girl, which upset Rachel – but the world could not stop at her horizon.

Six

I did not join Swan in his stealing but I observed him and thought about it. Who was it wronging? The boss of the big shop overcharged the customers, and could afford to lose the odd item. He never stole from small shops, no one had muddled his thinking by teaching him Right . . .

'Come over to my house,' I said to him one day. 'If she never sees you she'll think I invented you.'

He seemed amused. His own family did not think about him overmuch, and certainly never about his friends. 'What does she care?' he said. 'Anyway, she's seen me in the distance.' But he agreed to come, rather importantly, seeming pleased.

She was out, I showed him around. He was impressed that we had so much space. Space? Two rooms over a grocer, and the basement – a tiny hall and a patch of land? What about Wissingley with ten rooms and all the land outside – and he interrupted then and said, 'Oh that's a lot of crap, it's something you dreamed. It's your crazy side. Wissingley never happened, you probably lived in a shack.'

I glared at him. Then he added, 'You're a lying

geyser but I like it.' I was livid.

He looked at the bookshelves and said, 'She reads.'

'I've learnt a lot from her books.'

She reads. A statement like mentioning something peculiar, like saying: she is a deep-sea diver, a freak. Perhaps reading is a sort of deep-sea diving.

'I read too,' I said gingerly, daring to taunt his bogey.

'Fat lot of good it does, filling your head with ideas that don't apply and get you screwed.'

Was that true? Then his eye caught sight of a book with his name on it, he opened it and read, '*Du Côté de Chez Swann*', slowly and carefully, and he looked surprised.

'What's this about?' he asked.

'It's French.'

'So it's dirty.'

It was perhaps the first, last and only time in our short, intense life together that I felt superior – or at least adequate, not just Duddo.

'It's by a writer called Proust,' I said.

He gaped. 'Who's that then?'

'He wrote about Paris years ago when there were horse carriages and people wore orchids. There was a duchess and a kept woman –'

He interrupted, 'What's a kept woman, for Christ's sake? I always tell you not to talk funny. Like you are seventy or a bloody professor. *Who is Swann*?'

'Not your sort of swan.' But I was seventy now for him too, not just for Rachel – no longer too young.

He put the book back and said, 'So my name is real, I thought it was only a nickname. Like there is a book about me. Tell me about it. Can you read French?'

'We did French at my other school,' I said, starting to feel freakish, 'also at our school here, only you didn't bother. It was my mother who really taught me, she used to read aloud when we lived in the country. We didn't have telly. We were out of doors mostly all day, but in winter there were long afternoons and nothing else to do.'

'Tell me what happens to Swann.'

How could I tell a slam-banger like this Swan about the other one, even if I had read Proust properly, which I hadn't? I tried to tell him what James had explained to me, and – to my amazement and pleasure – Swan listened.

He had his head back and his eyes were half closed, and gradually I grew excited, as if something new was happening – for it was then that I saw the face he might have had if he'd been another sort of swan. If he hadn't opted out. Or maybe he had had no choice, his foreign family not settling down or being assimilated, keeping their ways that did not fit this city, and letting him run loose like a weed. People like Mother and James had shown me things – I realized for the first time what I had taken for granted, no one had tried to help Swan, who was still listening . . . I felt increasingly on the verge of a discovery, of a new dimension for us, that our friendship might be deeper. I trembled. Perhaps I could help him!

Suddenly he sat up and yawned, or pretended to yawn. The possibility passed, he didn't want it. He only cared because it was about his name. 'When is this mother of yours coming?' he asked, and our vital moment was over and lost.

'Let's go,' said Swan impatiently, suspicious

perhaps of a presence that had crept in, afraid of losing control, of my being in a position of equal footing.

'Your mother knows I'm real, she doesn't need to see me.'

He was too real now; I felt an enormous, enveloping disappointment.

'Wait a bit longer,' I said, 'I'll get you a drink. There's some whisky here. You don't have to get shirty; you *asked* me to tell you.'

'Well it's all balls.'

'Well you're a bore.'

'Well get the hooch.' He was boss again.

I fetched the bottle and rinsed some glasses left behind from Sam. I wondered what there was about reading that made him wary, almost as if he was frightened – that he tried to cover. There was a time when I had liked his apparent superiority, but – no longer. At Wissingley I had been an only child – Ashley and school were apart, and Gregg's son was a squealer of three we hardly ever saw, he spent his time in the farmyard with the cocks and hens. There had been no children to swipe my things or compete – I had received my mother's entire concentration . . . Perhaps it had been introspective in some ways – unimaginable to Swan . . . a parent actually to talk to . . .

She came in. He stared at her; they saw each other close for the first time. He became charming, shook her hand, very smooth and adult, though I could see that underneath he was ill at ease. We had been on the verge of a quarrel, the timing of her arrival had saved it. 'We were just leaving,' he said. 'How nice to meet you . . .' rather quickly – and we made the getaway he obviously wanted. We went off to join Suzy in a basement club in Fulham. On the way there all he said was, 'Some mother,' and I did not ask which way he meant it.

They got Swan. I learnt later from Suzy that it was in a big shop with closed-circuit-television detectors. He could have read the sign, only he never bothered to read anything, not even signs. For someone so clever, how stupid he had been.

Before Suzy told me this I had wondered where he was, as he had been missing for nearly a week – and I had been to see his family to ask if he was sick, he had never disappeared before.

There were seven people in one big room, an eighth person was behind a screen, crooning in a litany – he had an old man's voice. Swan had mentioned ten people – the others must have been out. It was another country. Swan's mother wore silk trousers and a shawl, her hair was like a rope, black and coarse, gleaming with oil that had a flowery smell; I found her beautiful. She nodded her head towards the curtain and said, 'He's praying, he wants to be alone.' I saw what Swan meant about us being lucky to have three rooms for two people.

He had been sent to a Youth Custody Centre. I asked what that was, and she told me 'a prison for the young'; so it was a polite name for Borstal.

'But – for only a minor offence?'

'It was not a first offence,' she said, her big gazelle's

eyes watering. How much was there that I did not know? Ill at ease – I fled.

After that I read and read, more than ever before. Perhaps it was in protest against Swan – he had been unfair about his family, his mother did think of him – but partly also because I had nothing to do. I read all the books that had been in our heavy suitcase years ago, all others acquired since, my mother's library books, everything I could find: Trollope, Amis, Donleavy, Meredith, Turgenyev, Iris Murdoch, Updike, Camus, Balzac, Graham Greene, Paul Scott, even Sartre . . . I grew desperate for something to do, and kept remembering Swan's mother and the old man praying. Was he praying for Swan to be let out – to see the light and change? What sort of God did he pray to, was it Vishnu? Buddha? (Not a *first* offence? What else had Swan done?)

I started to worry about money; without Swan I made none. I tried to sell my stamp album but was told it was worth only five pounds. I got out my old, once-loved butterfly collection from under the bed and tramped with it all the way to the British Museum, certain it was our treasure and would save us. They did not want it, but gave me advice: there were a few rare species, maybe worth a few pounds each – the whole thing might bring in twenty pounds.

On the way home I sat in the park; my shoes had rubbed and my feet hurt, but I liked walking. A child came and stared at the glass box that contained my emerald-green and bright-blue dreams. 'Here – have it,' I said on sudden impulse, and handed him my butterflies. His eyes opened wide, looking up at me in astonishment, not knowing if I meant it, a slightly trembling expression round his mouth that was not quite a smile. Then very carefully he took the box and went away. From the way he carried it I could see it would be cherished. I should have been pleased, but as it disappeared, it looked familiar and forlorn, a friend I had betrayed.

Things stagnated. Even though life with Swan may have been the negative of the photograph, without him there was no life at all. The Rachel and Suzy group also seemed to lack ideas and things to do, they hung about, rather idle. I tried some agencies for jobs, but I had no national-insurance card. The advertisements in the evening paper that the grocer always gave us did not suit my qualifications. What qualifications? I had no education, nor had I learnt a trade, I could not be a carpenter or a plumber . . . I just knew how to break in horses. I wanted to tell her I had left school, but not until I had a job. It might please her if I earned money, it might prevent her from urging me back to those fruitless studies. For a short time I delivered newspapers, but gave it up as the job started too early and I thought she would guess.

For a week I worked for a garage, filling petrol tanks and hand-washing cars. There were two mechanics there who had chips on their shoulders about foreign cars. 'Who cares if they're foreign,' I said, 'why not the best car for its own sake?' – and this remark immediately put a distance between us. They shared their views, I was different - not that they thought deeply about anything, most of the time they just swore, fuck, piss and shit, that summed it all up. When it rained it was either pissing or bloody. I once said, '*Bore* is a four-letter word too. It gets monotonous.' They gaped. 'Cor,' one of them said, 'and he's not even trained.' That had nothing to do with it, but they were right, they were trained mechanics and I suppose I sound square. I was sacked, probably for this reason, also the boss must have guessed I was school age. I had taken pleasure in polishing and waxing the cars and regretted not having kept my big mouth shut.

I walked all over London, still pretending I was at school, and so having to be out at school hours . . . walking on, hoping for a miracle such as running into James, the way Ma always ran into people. But evidently I was not like her, they were all strangers, staring into far distance, right through me as if I was transparent. I actually didn't show. How would I describe myself? Tawny hair, grey eyes, freckles - an average chap. Mr Nobody. I longed for a distinctive appearance, and I was wearing out my shoes, which annoyed me, my scuffed shoes would be a giveaway if I applied for another job - though many people wore scuffed gym shoes, I preferred moccasins, specially the ones the colour of conkers. Anyway - how could I apply for another job - where?

I was addicted to walking now and had to keep on; I

liked roaming the town and discovering new areas that I didn't know, it became an adventure. Once the police stopped me and asked where I was going. I said 'for a walk' and they were suspicious and searched my pockets. I used to think the police protective, but not after that. They let me go on my way, a harmless second-class citizen – but the next time I saw a policeman I felt guilty, as if I had done far worse than just miss school and lie to my mother. (At Wissingley, the local policeman used to call sometimes, to see if we were all right in our isolated house. He would drink tea with us and tell us about his family.)

At about half-past four in winter when the first twilight comes, the street lamps are lit and the sky turns an intense yet ethereal blue – the city seems to float and it grows beautiful. This luminous time between day and night always made me feel happy, even expectant. But it would alternate at other times, if I passed a take-away shop and there would be that filthy stench of whatever grease they use to cook with, which was the side of London I never got used to. I would sometimes even retch, and feel I did not belong, and crawl along looking at travel posters and wanting to go far away. I remembered James's tales, the way he described giant prawns grilled with garlic in Spain, or *mechoui* in Tunisia . . . I thought of my father living abroad and wondered where. At the time of the garage job, I had stopped seeing Rachel and her group, and the longer I left it, as the weeks passed, the more impossible it felt to get in touch. I wanted to go on somewhere new, not back. I spent many weeks on my walking marathon, going out each day, keeping on walking, looking strangers in the eye, wishing I might hold them like the Ancient Mariner, hoping for a glimmer of curiosity or recognition, praying someone would say, 'Hello old Tim.' No one did. But I carried a conviction inside me that things were going to change, or next luminous twilight I would burst . . . I knew *something had to happen.*

Seven

One day a lady from school came to see my mother. It was the English teacher I liked, a young woman with a long, blonde pigtail. She asked if my mother knew I had left school. Ma turned on me, furious, but before she could speak I said that if I had to go back there I would leave home. She sat down hard into a chair as if she had been hit, and rocked up and down like that crazy old wife of Gregg's, shaking her head. It was weird, I felt as if the walls of our house were soft and waving like in a surrealist painting I had seen with James.

'Old Tim,' she said after a while, very quiet, 'I didn't know it was that bad.'

This was hard. I would have preferred her angry, but was unable to move. The teacher became active and made some tea and said let's have a talk and call me Sally. She broke the tension slightly, I gave a nervous laugh that sounded false and said to my mother, 'Don't blame anyone except Nettlebed, it's all his fault. If we have to blame someone, let's not make it each other.'

'Who's Nettlebed?' asked Sally.

'My dad.'

We drank tea and were polite. The teacher said it was a shame because I had been an eager pupil (she was wrong, it was only that I found her pretty) and that maybe she could give me private lessons and see if she could coax me back.

My mother sighed, she started to cry and then she laughed and looked peculiar. 'You are kind,' she said. 'I would not have forced him. What a waste. I did so hope he would have an education and pass his exams.'

I had not known she worried about me.

'I would like to help,' said Sally.

'Why should you?'

'It's my job. I like teaching. The young don't seem to want to learn in this generation: it is rare to find a boy who is interested.'

There was a silence. I was intrigued and realized this would be something to do. 'Could I come to your house for lessons?' I asked on a sudden impulse. 'It is rather claustrophobic here.' Seeing my mother's face, I felt terrible – too late – but she had always been fair to me, so I added, 'It isn't you Ma, it's these lovers and people who come here. There isn't really room for me too . . .'

Sally looked at her, Ma blushed and drew herself up, becoming remote. Her face grew expressionless. She said, cool and dignified, 'Thank you Miss Sally. This boy longs to learn. Or used to. I have neglected him maybe. When we first came here we went to the Natural History Museum and saw whales' skeletons, but I got involved with city life and he grew older. I suppose I let him drift.'

I couldn't remember the whales' skeletons. But I

thought: neglect? She taught me more before we came here than I have learned ever since.

'It's serious,' my mother said. 'He's fifteen. Sixteen soon. Take him.'

She turned away, probably deliberately, we were dismissed. We went. But once down the steps and outside, she suddenly came and stood in the doorway and watched us off. I was only going to a teacher's house for a lesson, I wasn't going away on a journey, but the way she stood there I might have been carrying an aeroplane bag.

My mother has black hair, it is fine and soft – in the sunlight it has a reddish sheen as if she has a wild animal inside her that does not always show, the red can only be seen in a strong light. It was late afternoon, the time the sun hits that side of our street, the time the traffic jam starts, nearly time for Sam, though he didn't come every night because he had a wife. The sunset was showing the red in her hair that Sam had never seen, but I suppose he found out about her wild side in bed at night.

'I saw a bear dancing once,' said my mother, switching right off as if she was just a little queer, with that faraway face she had for the old world that had been beautiful and the things that don't happen any more. 'Bears used to travel with their owners and dance in villages. Goodbye Timmy.'

We waved goodbye, though I would be back for dinner; it was goodbye to a certain period of our life, and I always remember her standing in that flame light looking into the distance, seeing me off – and my real manhood started for me then as we walked down the street. Maybe Ma felt it somewhere in her intuition.

'So why don't bears dance in villages any more?' I asked Sally, rather excited by the adventure of her surprise visit. 'Why can't we have a better world without losing the old things?'

'Too much traffic for bears,' said Sally. 'It was in the days when there were hardly any cars, no television, live entertainment like puppet shows and travelling clowns. People with leisure. I am surprised your mother can remember, she must have lived in primitive countryside. Where was it?'

'She never told me.'

'How strange you both are. It must have been a place with little transport.'

'*Easy* transport has ruined everything!' I shouted. She made me want to talk. 'It should take long and be difficult to go somewhere, then it is fun, and unspoiled when you arrive.'

'You are a funny, old-fashioned boy,' she said, looking at me sideways.

She was a friend at once, I had never chattered so easily before on first meeting a person. 'The old people remember the world was beautiful – up until the last war I am told. Now there are package tours to go and join a lot of other tourists on a beach and only one real fisherman left, I've seen it on television. Magical Mystery Tour of Yugoslavia – then see

Dubrovnik with tall modern buildings like Tottenham Court Road.'

From the first moments with her, any subject, great or small, would disclose a new view – like opening a window and finding a landscape outside that you had not known was there, because your eyes did not see it; she produced an extra dimension, a change of focus.

'Pop songs about being on the road with a suitcase and nowhere to go annoy me,' I went on, carried away. 'We didn't need to go anywhere, we had a place, Sally, an old house under the moors with curlews wailing outside like spirits – eerie in a way – but life was . . . well, you could feel it and smell it and breathe it . . .'

She understood immediately about our house – and then we reached hers. We climbed a staircase with torn linoleum; there was a smell of cooking. A door on the second landing opened and a wrinkled old man looked out. Her flat was on the top floor and when we got inside the fusty smell disappeared. There was a bed, two chairs, a table, a sofa, records and books, and a bunch of leaves and branches in a jug. I started looking through her records and could not stop chattering.

'It's become an easy lifestyle to be a drop-out or a misfit,' I said, 'a trend.'

'But *you* are a misfit.'

'Then I'm a bore.' But I turned quickly to see whether she meant it or was teasing: she looked thoughtful and I noticed her eyes were green.

'No,' she said, 'you're not a bore. You're not a drop-out either – you're a drop-back . . . you revert to what was before. At school I noticed you fought ideas,

I thought: he cares in a way the others don't. I realized then that you must have been brought up differently, in an unusual way, perhaps even an obsolete way, and I wondered . . .'

'So I'm a dinosaur.'

'You are outside category. I hoped you might be the new generation . . . there *are* signs of change in the world.'

'May I touch your hair? It has lights that glitter . . .'

'I can't place you, I've never met people like you and your mother.'

My hand trembled. It happened sharp as a thunder-clap: this was the first time I truly wanted a woman. Anything I had known or done previously faded, I was strong and grown, a different being, an enormous feeling welling up inside me. All earth's rivers started running at cross currents, carrying the moon into the ocean and out to the edge of the world.

So began my grown life, the first woman I had met who was not my mother and not a randy teenager like poor Rachel and her squalid friends. Sally was like the books I had read, and she was a teacher of all things: we studied, we discussed writers, a universe existed in her room, my new world, Donne's Newfoundland. While I wrote essays she would undo her pigtail and shake her hair loose and smoke small, thin cigars, lying on the sofa, and we would talk and sleep and wake together, and I started to love her . . . her mind, her long body, everything about her; I loved her bare room, the magic bunch of mixed leaves, the striped teapot. I had to be close to her even when we were reading, to hold her hand and feel part of her touching me and electric, I could not exist without her. We read new things, Lorca, the history of Spain, Hugh Thomas on the civil war, Ortega y Gasset on Andalusia. 'You will take your A-levels,' she said. We read the French poets, Baudelaire and Rimbaud, it was an adventure, the strong black tea she made was earth's blood. I was burning with the excitement of learning at the same time as having her, we would stop working and lie wrapped in each other's arms and see the stars. She would look at me with her long green eyes, teasing me as an adolescent, wanting me as a man.

She took me to a French movie at the National Film Theatre, about a schoolteacher who has an affair with a young boy. It was called *Le Diable au corps* and it ended sadly. 'We must never end,' I said, but she only answered, 'Oh God I wish you were older - though perhaps if you were it wouldn't be so strong.'

I told her about James, who had also taken me to the South Bank to see *Raimu* - I loved old black-and-white movies. I wished she could meet James. Where was he now? Would Ma be jealous? It was more likely that I would be.

Sally liked lentils, the dark-green sort she said she could only find in Soho, and brown rice and chick-peas. She put sunflower seeds into her salads; they were delicious, I bought some packets and took them home. 'What are you now, a parrot?' said Ma.

I loved London now, I didn't care where I was as long as Sally was there. Wissingley slipped away and stopped mattering, but she said, 'Guard it preciously and one day something will grow out of it,' and she added that one day our time together would be over but that Wissingley must remain. To keep inside; the tree of life I had grown from. I thought our time could never be over – but she knew that 'forever' can be in the present tense, a feeling of touching eternity. She was the sky, the Northern Lights. I understood now how my mother felt about Sam because I went mad, crazy about Sally, but she gave me fulfilment, whereas Sam gave my mother torment. Sally was there when I needed her, she didn't drive off in the night and leave me to take sleeping pills.

My mother said, 'You don't beef about Wissingley any more now that you are interested in your lessons.'

'It's growing moss,' I said, 'I'll plant a tree there for you one day, Ma.'

Sally had made me tolerant and kinder – I understood how people can be mean to each other without realizing. I was not angry about Sam any more, but irritated with him man to man because he was a taker and my mother was a giver – but evidently this could not be helped.

'She seems to have settled you, she's a good teacher,' said my mother, which made me laugh. It was a good tutorial system.

'She sure is.'

I felt I had lived three years in three weeks – after I

met her everything changed. I tidied my room (and regretted the butterflies which I could not show her) – I went out occasionally with my mother, who bought me a new suit and a leather jacket; I had grown taller. She also seemed more settled herself, for when Sam did not come she did not pace about, she knew he would come another day. Our house regained its peace.

'What lies!' she exploded one day, watching television. At Wissingley we had probably been the only people in England who did not have a set; in London she watched it but it often made her cross. ' "Neat-a-pac tastes like home!" It's frozen sawdust.'

'It's only commercials,' I said. 'No need to get in a stew.'

'Why don't they make real stew?'

'They can't be bothered. Whether travelling or eating, they're in a hurry. They eat prefabricated food like their thoughts – swallowing down ready-made ideas like vitamin capsules, brainwashed – don't realize they aren't thinking for themselves . . .'

She looked surprised. 'Well at least you seem to be thinking for yourself. Quite assured, aren't you, old Tim? What are you thinking of all the time, since you know your thoughts?'

'Sex,' I said.

'Really?'

'Really. Everything reminds me of sex.'

'Everything?'

'Anything. Floods in the headlines, hailstorms, good shoes. Specially shoes, very sexy.'

'You must have just discovered it.'

I nearly said, you must have just discovered it too –

but refrained – she had had her past or I wouldn't be here. But I did say, 'What goes on in this house would make anyone think.'

She liked that, threw her head back and laughed. Three weeks ago she would not have done so, nor would I have said what I just said, it would have stayed inside, my corrosion, my smouldering resentment against Sam, my green copper heart.

The programme she was watching now changed to an advisory talk for the young, a message to choose a partner and so not catch AIDS. She turned it off and sighed.

'How tragic,' she said. 'So sad it has to become matter-of-fact, practical and flat . . .'

'Some people never find real love,' I said. 'That programme is for searchers who sleep around.'

'Goodness, you are a wise, old, old man, Timmy,' she said, and it was my turn to laugh, for I was old now even for her. No longer too small, someone left outside in the hall when important matters were discussed: her grown son.

I did the shopping. I respected her, and had learned it was foolish to try to understand another person or judge what might be best for them . . . Life settled into a pleasant groove. We were happy.

And then they let Swan out.

Eight

He was thinner and older. We set out for the evening, unsuccessfully pretending it was like the old days, which of course it was not. It had been nearly a year – he was eighteen – I had lost him somewhere. We joined Suzy and her hangers-on at a pub, it was a warm evening and they were sitting outside, and Suzy seemed even more unreal to me than Swan, yet there was a sameness and stale quality of familiarity that was embarrassing – I was so keen not to have belonged with them, depressed to think I had once done so – yet had I ever been truly one of them? – or was I always the outsider (the prig) . . .?

Then – standing alone by the doorway – there was my reminder: Rachel. As soon as I saw her particular outside-the-world aura I realized she had got off grass on to bigger things, and wondered who had started her and how it had happened. How long had Swan been out? I looked carefully at his elegant clothes which showed he must be making good money; I also saw that he had needle marks in an unusual place, the soft part of his hands between the thumb and forefinger. I should have kept quiet, but I asked him *why*.

'Why what?' annoyed.

'You know what I mean.'

He looked at me then with an unfriendly, rather blank gaze, the pupils of his eyes dilated like a wild dog's (his fix was probably wearing off), and he said, 'Because I want more, it's not enough.'

'More what?'

'To live more. Bigger. Have more of it. Just MORE you shit,' he shouted, working himself up to become nasty, his voice now petulant.

Somebody screamed; I saw that it was Rachel, slumped on the dirty pavement, sitting with her head hanging over her knees. She was sobbing, 'Leave me alone . . . don't touch me' – though nobody was touching her. They stood about gawking at her and each other doing nothing, in a trance, as if they didn't register or were listening to music from some other planet. Was this 'more'? I never liked drugs because people sail off on their own. They start together when the needle pricks but then fly. Alcohol is different. It's exciting.

Poor old Rachel. Poor cheese sandwich, she was a nice girl who could be a good wife, a pram-pusher. I felt suddenly a great tenderness for her, for the first time and too late. She didn't even recognize me – or maybe she hadn't looked. Don't touch me anyway. Screaming not to be touched, but really it was: help, how did I get here. And yobbos watching with sightless eyes, only seeing their own projection. Young men leaning propped up on any lamp post – any doorway, deep in a strange absence. From the distance it could be a normal group of people outside a pub on an ordinary evening – but in truth I had stumbled into quicksand.

Then I hated Swan. Taking dope was his business, but it was clear he was pushing the hard stuff, that was where his clothes came from, and the banknotes. He had taught Rachel what she had not asked to know, so that afterwards she needed it and ended up slobbering on the pavement, old at seventeen.

'Good night,' I said to Swan. 'You're just a lousy pusher. Are these your great plans? You'll get five years next time.'

'What are *your* plans then? Are you making any money, Mr Right? You're a stupid fucker and always were.'

I walked away, leaving no reflection in the opaque panes of his eyes.

Before I reached the end of the street I saw two policemen approaching the group (which did not look so innocuous after all) and I stopped and waited. One of them asked questions, the other one wrote on a pad. Probably Rachel was now a junkie with rations, a name on a list, she and the others, isolated non-people.

The police looked from Swan to me and then beckoned. I returned and was questioned, Swan said I was his friend, looking peculiarly victorious and illogical, considering our recent farewell. That was all, I went off again but would have done better to have kept going instead of feeling some misplaced loyalty.

★

I started to trek down North End Road, past Fulham Broadway . . . St Stephen's Hospital . . . towards our home where Sam and my mother seemed to be each other's drug, and as I walked I wondered about Swan's way and many other things. Ma must be naturally turned-on, she used to go wild for old trad jazz, dance and fling her clothes off. As a small child I was brought up – probably unconsciously – to think it normal to leap about half naked, that clothes were restrictive. We saw so few people in the country and there were no rules. But she was lawless. I passed the Marsden Hospital and remembered the way she sang on horseback, galloping Nero and shouting a Russian cavalry song that her grandfather had apparently taught her. Was this the feeling Swan was looking for? I had read that Aldous Huxley took mescalin as an experiment. Swan had been my idol once. It was all ahead then, his plans were going to bring glory . . . Now Rachel had violet hair, which should add to her personality . . . but before she had had many natural colours finely shaded in her funny mouse-mop, it had been more subtle.

I was approaching a yellow brick building that had '1927' sculpted in stone over the doorway. Ma was not even born then. How old was she anyway? I didn't know if she was thirty-eight or forty-eight but she was certainly having a long, hot summer. I wondered if her time was running out. She had told me Bix Beidebecke had died of loving his music so much he did not look after himself and was burned out at both ends, 'the young man with a horn'. Had he died of drugs? Wasn't she burning at both ends, in a different way? She said it was a nice way for him to die, to go out on a crescendo. I used to accept and learn from all she said, she seemed to be an expert on crescendos. Was it just luck, whether you found your person? Sally listened to jazz but quite differently: she did not dance, she sat still as if hypnotized, she liked Earl Hines and Django Reinhardt.

Now I passed the mansion block where Ma used to go and read to a blind lady, but gave it up when she met Sam - and I turned into our street. James had suggested that I become a naturalist. My time was running out too, I was getting nowhere in spite of studying with Sally - I must take my O-levels and A-levels like she said, and must hurry, I had left it late . . . but my thoughts kept returning to Swan. He reared up in front of me like a cobra, his beautiful tall body in his purple velvet trousers, his motionless eyes gone-still with hash, my first city friend, the opposite of Ashley, replacement of Ashley, the ugly expression now spoiling his face. Not to think of him. Anyone else. Gregg's wife then; who looked after her fits now? Sally said she must be an epileptic or an alcoholic with delirium tremens. Another person needing 'more'? (I could hear the wind blowing across the moors, ruffling the leaves in the little copses, and the yelping screams of vixens in heat.) I had told Sally how Ma managed to soothe Gregg's woman and took trouble, but if the vicar of our village suggested a coffee morning, she bolted. We were all bolters from something. To escape - but also to *find.* How was Jake? He must be growing old . . . Sally said pedigree cats lived less long than alley cats. He must have settled in all this time, I could never take him back now . . .

I opened our front door; inside the hall I could hear her voice on the telephone. She was saying, 'I miss you so much when you can't come, it's as if my body will break.' So she wanted 'more' too in her fashion – but suffering seemed to be part of their dimension. I didn't hate Sam any more, I disliked him because it was habit, tanned on to my skin – but he was part of me. Sam was my ingrown toenail. What I resented was the compromise that took him home at night, to the other person he also cheated, it was somehow unworthy. Though I was tired now, this thought made me turn round and go out again, I wanted to tell Sally about what had happened to Swan, suddenly there was a lot to discuss. Poor Ma after all, and poor Sam, they could only have a few nights a week and she could not go to his house on impulse to talk . . . That was why people quaked and roared and felt empty and wanted more . . .

Sally had a little car and once we went away for the weekend; it was the first time I had been back to the country since Wissingley and I was smitten. We went to a village in the Cotswolds where she knew a small inn, we had a room at the back and lay in bed in the morning hearing rooks in a great clump of trees. I loved her for giving me this, though the fact that she had to pay annoyed me. The smell of the earth outside and the way the air was clean made me feel like an animal, I wanted to roll. But when we had dinner in the dining room I found it rather false and could not quite explain why. They weren't real country people, they were city people pretending – and though the countryside where we walked was pretty, it felt small.

She said that was the way of the south – that the north was vast and with a panache as great as Spain, and I learned that she came from Yorkshire, her home had been in a black-and-white village where her parents still lived – so she was really a country person too, like me. Only she had loved the city from the first moment of her arrival, the big shops, the exhibitions and libraries, the bustle. I asked whether she went back to see her parents; she said that after settling in London it felt rather blank in her old home, specially since her two brothers had gone to America – but she did go sometimes for Christmas. And as she spoke of these things, she started to tell me about a village called West End which was tiny and surrounded by moors where there were curlews, about Fountains Hall where the heirs, a brother and sister, were both killed in the war and there was no one left to inherit, but their statues were standing outside, still young and in uniform . . . about Ripon where the pews were carved with heads of strange animals – when she was a child a horn was blown every night at the market cross in this town . . . She grew enthusiastic and started to tell me about food, how it was different in the north too – so excellent that before the industrial revolution one of the kings of France had had an English chef – the best ham in France is still called *jambon d'York*. Then I put my hand over her chattery mouth and said, 'We aren't having lessons about the industrial revolution now, teacher,' and I held her warm body tight, so tight, I wished we could die together; how could I ever give all of myself or have enough of her –

or ever assuage the longing for beyond and beyond always farther . . .?

We only had two days. She gave me a driving lesson in a little lane. I was hooked and giggled hilariously and swerved all over the grass verges but would not stop. I felt magnificent. Possessive. The master. We bought honey and home-made cakes to take back to London. We visited the haunted ruin of Minster Lovell with the peculiar statue Sally thought was perhaps supposed to be Richard III, and the smooth turf sloping down to the clear water of the River Windrush where they used to wash the wool; and in Burford the gravestones of the sheep farmers which had scrolls of twisted wool skeins sculpted in stone round their edges.

I did see that, though it was doll's-house land, the village where we stayed – the houses of beautiful stone, and people mowing the lawns of their tiny gardens and talking to each other over the walls – had a sort of cosiness, under the lee of the short-view hills outside where we walked.

It was a let-down to return to London. I stood in the doorway looking at our unmade bed, at the room where I had really lived with her – not just visited. I wanted to keep it indelible, wrapped in the green smell of mown grass, the smell of her hair, her skin.

Nine

One night when dinner was ready, a little bunch of flowers on the table and the Beaune 1982 uncorked, Sam did not come – and this night was not their usual vague arrangement, he was definitely expected.

She sat waiting, very quiet, beside the fire in the little hob grate where she burned logs, though we lived in a smokeless zone (woodsmoke never hurt anyone, she said, better than bus fumes), staring into the flames, and waited, and went on waiting. Then drew her shawl tighter. He was an hour late, then two hours, something must have happened. She started rocking the chair and she started to talk, and for the first time in the years that had passed it was of Wissingley that she spoke. Until now it had been like a room with the door closed where someone had died.

'Remember that old bathtub, Timmy,' she said, 'the way the overflow opened direct through the wall, so when you lay in the bath the wind would come in and howl and you would be lying there in hot water all safe?'

'Yes,' I said. I had been the nagging one but had stopped long ago and I hated this. I could have pretended to be dense, to have forgotten – she had never played my game at the time, so why now?

'Remember the larder, how the airing hole opened straight out of the roof, like a chimney – so when you went in to fetch the butter you would hear larks singing overhead, as if they were in the store cupboard?'

'Yes,' I said, 'I remember every single stone, and I hate remembering and don't want to talk about it.'

'He's not coming,' she said.

'No, Ma, not tonight.'

We sat and waited, and she went on staring into the fire.

'Why is it you like him so,' I asked then, 'why him and not James?'

She roused herself slightly. 'I don't mind James,' she said. 'One can love two people.'

'So you might end up with him after all?' I asked, brightening.

'He never asked me to *end up* with him,' she said, unexpectedly laughing.

'You didn't give him much chance.'

'Park bench more likely. I still love James in a way, but after Sam I couldn't bear him to touch me.'

I poured out some whisky and gulped it down.

'What is it about Sam, Ma?'

Her voice sounded very soft. 'Who can explain? He's wild.'

'But you don't want to sleep out on the moors, do you, till you die in the gale?'

'I don't know. I don't know. Maybe I do.'

There was silence, and I poured her some whisky too. She was thinking he still might come and I was praying he would not, back to my old suspicion and dislike of the way he took possession and upset our life, mine as well as hers.

'Sam is deadly nightshade,' I told her. 'You just said you liked the hot bath at Wissingley with the storm locked outside. James is safe, meadow grass, or maybe that redwood tree that was so strong.'

'Lightning struck it.'

I had forgotten. I hoped lightning would now strike Sam's car and that he would have an accident, or maybe had already. The whisky and her stubbornness were continuing to bring back my old rage. I moved nearer and held her hand because I was sorry for her, it was my turn now to be strong. Her hand was cold and she was trembling. Was Sam what she had looked for all her life, galloping on Nero, excited by danger (for Nero could be lethal too), or was she oblivious – out running with her butterfly net but not to catch butterflies, like me – she hoped to catch stars, the dreamer, the fool . . . I had been that way once but the city had changed me, I was solid and square, Wissingley remained inside sprouting practical shoots out of its moss, like wanting her to have James and be protected, but seeing that the member of the family who must prepare a place for her later should be me. Growing old should be just a season. Her long, hot summer might still be turning into a warm October with a rainbow light, but November would come and she was heading for a cold one.

Suddenly impatient I shouted, 'All right! So stop it!'

'What?' She jumped.

'So he isn't coming. So to hell. Wake up Ma, you're

being a drag. I am going upstairs to change into my new suit, I am a guest coming to dinner and you'd better treat me right – I want interesting conversation – we're not going to sit here moping – remember Mope? That was your slogan. Nineteen-eighty-two is a good year for Beaune, James said so, and we're going to enjoy it.'

She threw off the shawl, warm with the fire and the whisky, and she said, 'Hurry then, Timmy, and come back *new*. And pour me another while I wait, and put on a Bix Beiderbecke record and –' I was gone.

Ten minutes later I went outside and rang the doorbell. She opened the door flushed and with shining eyes.

'I understand a beautiful lady lives here and has asked me over,' I said.

'There's no lady here, but come on in, tramp.' And we rushed down to the basement and lit the candles, and she drew the curtains saying, 'We don't want the werewolves looking in.'

'Werewolves . . .' I said. 'What were those tales based on I wonder?'

'Men who change after dark.'

'They sure change after dark round here.' In fact Sam only ever comes after dark, I thought, or in first dusk. What does he look like in the daylight? Creatures of the night, the owl and the bat.

'Did they dress up as wolves, do you think?'

'Why not? All the better to eat you, of course.'

'That was a wolf dressed as a person, not a werewolf . . .'

But either way – of course. A normal three-star dinner in a good restaurant. I thought of the Canadian timber wolves she had taken me to see at Whipsnade, running in a pack, even in their small pinewood – tails out, restless, some ancient instinct making them lope in a team behind the leader. In Canada they probably covered hundreds of miles. Here they still darted upwind, noses twitching. 'Did you know wolves are loyal animals?' Ma had said at the time, looking at them excitedly (she probably associated them with Sam). 'They kill to eat, but never each other. They mate for life.'

We sat down at the table and had a wonderful dinner of the roast beef in rosemary that she had prepared for Sam, miraculously not overdone – and that I would have had cold for breakfast. I ate with particular relish like a crow eating Sam's corpse, only we were more like two lapwings in reeling air currents, coasting and swerving on the wind, chattering and laughing, and when the Beaune ran out we continued with Bull's Blood and Talegio cheese and were filled with creative ideas. She found strange chords on the old piano; we sang.

Then she said, 'Let's go into the garden,' and out we clambered, by this time in a *vino veritas* dream, we were wild with happiness, even if she was feeling a no-Sam place on another level. It was an evening of discovery, the songs we had sung, a new idea she had for a tune, now she started pruning the jasmine, cutting it back and scolding it, telling it to grow in a different direction, laughing and almost crying. I thought: slow down or you'll miss the corner – I can feel the edge coming. Those Canadian wolves with the north wind in their memories, going back to all the wolves that went before, even penned in, they don't lose their primeval north. Is that where the heart is, or is it in the stomach? I went indoors to fetch the bottle, to have a drop more whisky neat in very small glasses, like a liqueur – to be quaffed outside in the balmy air with the traffic murmur beyond the garden wall like a beast breathing. King Leopard the wicked city night. Us safe in our dappled vines and leaf-patterns.

The jasmine leaned into the next-door garden; she peered through and came head-on with the neighbour who was doing the same. There he was, a man literally materialized out of leaves, and us on our side, me with a grocer's crate caught and snapping under one foot.

We had never met our neighbour, and now he was suddenly watching us leaping in our garden, like mad deer. He was called Arthur, he said, and she said, 'Oh do climb the fence and come and join us.' So he came into our basement and we danced, each of us separate and swaying round on our own, but it was a party. Keep Sam away, I thought. Make Arthur a new friend. Let someone, anyone, get this thing unhooked. If we were ill in the night, would Arthur come to our aid? We had been here all this time and never met him. He would be away for the weekend. Oh . . . man is the loneliest animal, lonelier than the beasts in Whipsnade, taught to go against his instincts . . . and I recalled that zoo emu, so old, so mad, it had forgotten about being lonely or where it came from, disgruntled and snoring with asthma in the wrong climate . . . I was getting confused ideas, so I made some coffeee and left them and went upstairs. I needed to be alone. Maybe she would get on well with the new man . . . or was he an emu? It was fascinating, there really were two hand rails, two door knobs at the top, even two toothbrushes.

I had a bath and thought of wind through the drainpipe and larks in the larder and wondered about the sense behind it all. Was there a pattern? As a child I had asked her about God and whether she thought her parents knew what was happening to us (I knew they were dead). She only said, 'When people have gone I doubt if they lean out of the sky listening to our conversations.' Then were they up in the sky? She said no one knew, they just hoped. She wasn't very forthcoming on that subject. In fact we had never read the Bible. I wondered what was behind the visible world. Where, now, was the great faith that had inspired the men who made the stained-glass windows in cathedrals? *He who would valiant be*, we used to sing at school with Ashley, clasping our hymnals. I loved the music, and Bunyan's words, *'gainst all disaster*. I wondered if Sally thought God was sad. What a mess man had made . . . the ozone layer . . . the hole in the sky . . . I slipped in the bath, then clambered out, reached my bed and sank into it still wet. A framed prayer that hung on the wall of Sally's kitchen floated into my vision: *you are a child of the universe, no less than the trees and the stars, you have a right to be here* . . . the lights from cars in the street made zebra stripes move across the ceiling . . . I heard Ma come upstairs singing her new tune; she went straight to her room and did not take pills which I knew were kept in the bathroom. A wonderful evening . . . maybe we were rid of Sam.

In the morning we had tremendous hangovers, with heads like gongs, but also an ethereal feeling that was happy, the aftermath of the evening lingered on, it had left a sharp perception yet a feeling of floating. We sat in the basement drinking black coffee and I took the opportunity of this pleasant haze to ask, 'Why do you never talk of the past? Are you hiding something?'

'Hiding?'

'Then why?'

She looked slightly surprised, then thoughtful. After a while she said, 'The saddest day of my life was when I left home. I suppose I have just never wanted to talk about it, old Tim. It receded and became unreal. What was the point?' But she leaned back in her chair and continued quietly, 'My parents were killed in a car crash. I adored my grandfather who lived with us – but I was sent away. "Why can't I stay here and live with you?" I kept asking, but he said an old man could not cope with a young girl who must grow up – and that it was out of his hands, they had arranged to send me to a cousin in Chicago. Who were "they"? My tutor, who was also my guardian I suppose – and the distant cousin. I was ten years old. All I knew was that I was never to return – and I ran about all over the garden clutching at mossy stones, branches of lilac, it was spring, it was drenched in the smell of flowers – were my parents *under* this earth now? Where were they? . . . "You will write to me, won't you?" Grandpa said . . . only I never did because there were only sad things to tell him and I didn't want him to know. Later on when I heard he had died I was tortured with remorse. Death cuts you off completely, you can't talk to the person any more, or explain all those possible misunderstandings. Nor can you ask questions of their knowledge – because they had taken their *mind* with them. No one can understand about death until it happens to them. The day I had left, in the car with my suitcase, he had waved goodbye and said, "So I won't see you grow up after all . . ." Oh God, I thought later when I heard he had gone, did he think I didn't love him because I didn't write? Please know I loved you, Grandpa. It's got to *get through* . . . to *reach* you. But there was only a void, and no answer.'

Her voice sounded sad and started fading away. All these years later it still made her cry.

'Go on Ma,' I said, 'I would like to know where I came from. The people you met here who knew you from Chicago must have reminded you . . . and now we have got started . . .'

'Ah well then,' she resumed, 'I was an only child and lived with my parents and grandfather in Radnorshire.'

'Is that where the bear danced?'

'Yes, one Christmas. A huge bonfire on the village

green and swans cracking the ice on the pond, pushing it with their strong breasts and hitting it with their beaks . . . and snow . . . and church bells ringing.'

'That is a good memory then.'

'Yes indeed, a special one. But the same bells tolled later for my parents. We had a rambling old house and a big farm; it was remote from what my parents called good schools and they didn't believe in boarding school, so I had a tutor. He was afraid of twilight, he said it was the time when the swamp fairies came out of the mist and took people away. I suppose he taught me a reasonable amount . . . literature and French . . . and he gave me the desire to read. We had horses, my father was interested in cross-breeding sheep, but I knew no children, we were far from the village which was tiny anyway. I was taught to ride young, almost as soon as I could walk . . . I knew animals better than people. My grandfather was a splendid horseman, even at eighty he would ride the whole estate each day. And when I was ten – suddenly this all ceased. My parents skidded one night coming home from a dinner, they went into a tree and the car caught fire, probably because they carried extra jerry cans of petrol in the boot. It was arranged for me to go to my only relative, a cousin of my mother's who was a professor at Chicago University. I had never been away, even to London, and had never met anyone outside home and the village. Chicago sounded like another planet. When I got there . . . the professor-cousin was detached and very cold, an abstract intellectual, his wife was a shrew, probably annoyed to be stuck with a young girl – I don't know – but she called me clodpole and I certainly wasn't wanted. I ran away. They never tried to find me.'

She picked up the coffee pot but it was empty.

'I'll make some more in a minute,' I said.

'Well, I got a job on the stage, I was fourteen by then – a hoofer in musicals in the chorus line – when I was sixteen I started singing.' (She sounded now as if she was hurrying through a book and skipping the chapters.) 'Then I got a part in a play and became interested in drama, I read a great deal, from Molière and Racine to Eugene O'Neill and Tennessee Williams. Your father was sitting in the audience one night and came backstage afterwards and invited me to dinner. He was half Egyptian, half English, he used the same expressions of speech as my father and my tutor, he seemed like the landscape I had left behind. He was also glamorous. Maybe I loved him – or did I think he would keep me safe, we would be a family again . . .? I don't know. But we married. And he was jealous. So jealous it was sick. After you were born I had to have sitters when I was acting, because he wasn't going to stay at home with you, he wanted to keep a check on me. He sat through every performance and could not bear men in the audience to look at me. He gave me no money, so apart from loving to act, I also had to earn. Our life became a persecution. He would storm into the manager's office and make scenes, he thought I was having an affair with the leading man. He argued with the director that I must give up my part. When he was told I showed promise and had a future career he punched the man in the nose. It was ridiculous and quite mad, but also dreadful. Melodrama is boorish.

He became so much of a nuisance that I was fired.'

She sighed and then said impatiently, 'Why on earth do we have to talk of this?'

'Because it is where I came from,' I said. 'So I am English, a quarter Egyptian and born in America. We won't have to go over it again but I do think I had a right to know. In fact, *damn* it.'

'Sorry, old Tim, of course you did. But in the beginning, when we got to Wissingley, you were just a little fellow and I wanted to show you the sun and the moon. Then it became all buried and gone. You are older now, it is different. I was shattered to find how arid his heart was . . . and that he was a miser – yet he could sometimes be so nice – I hoped and hoped and was sorry for him. Pity is a killer. Anyway I got a divorce.'

'And Wissingley, how did that come about?'

'His lawyer informed me that you and I could go and live in a place your father had inherited but did not want – lost in wild countryside – that we must leave Chicago at once, for he never wanted to see us again.'

'A psychopath.'

'I was told he would pay for your school and the rates and expenses on the house, but would give us no other money. He must have thought it was a punishment. He had told the lawyer I was guilty of flirting with the theatre director, of not giving up my career. An absurd attitude – lucky he never realized the truth or he might have thought up some other solution – I mean he thought we were banished to the back of beyond! Whereas, though it was rough till we got organized – you and I had the best life we could have had, old Tim, as I hope you will always remember. I was so pleased to get away from him I did not contest any of the arrangements or ask for money. He paid the fare. We arrived in Wissingley . . . it was derelict, damp . . . and we were home. I could ride again, and teach you also – it was like being born again on the moors, Gregg's farm a few miles away . . .'

She went off silently again into some other dream of her own. I got up and started to make us a real breakfast with fruit juice and toast. I wondered if she had missed her acting. She must have held back many things. Maybe she *had* gone to bed with Erskine or the director, that was her affair . . . only I would have been intrigued to know if one of them was the fellow she met in the street who had offered her a movie job.

I brought the coffee and laid out the cups and plates.

'I loved Wissingley even more than my own old home,' she said then, 'because it was happy from the start. In a way, we made it, we built it up from a wreck. And you see . . . when my parents were killed, I saw them. I hope you never see a burnt person. They were buried in our village churchyard, you can visit their graves one day if you want to. My mother was killed instantly but my father lived on two days. I remember him shivering in bed, he was so cold, I kept putting more and more blankets on him, I kept saying, "I love you Papa, I'll mend you with my love," and was surprised that he seemed in a state of anxiety about small things, like his watch or the time or the glass of water by the bed or the medicine. I didn't understand, and as the years passed and I grew older I kept thinking about it. Eventually I decided it must have been a desperate attempt to hold on to visible things, to hold the world down and not leave it, not let it go . . . to cling to familiar objects, the clock, the furniture. Why should he want to die? He was only forty-five.'

'What were your parents like?'

'I remember Mama as rather dreamy – in the evenings she wore chiffony things – long beads. Father was dark. I think they were much in love because they rarely went out, just occasionally to local friends – they would drive off thirty miles for dinner – but otherwise they read a great deal and had huge discussions. My father was busy, he had a big farm to run, though with a manager. When he lay in his bed dead, and so still, I remember my hot tears all over him – but he was too cold to warm any more . . . I did have a happy childhood, though, till it was disrupted. Socrates said, "Give me a child until it is seven and I will form it for life." '

'Damn Socrates!' I interrupted angrily, 'I don't agree. Eight or ten is a fatal time for major events. Look what happened to us both! Most families have Aunt Agathas that knit, we have both been solitaries.'

'All the same, we have managed.'

'What did we live on?' I asked then.

'My music,' she said. 'The pieces I wrote were bought; I had the remains of theatre contacts when we arrived from America. It was not well paid, but we had our own vegetables – and eggs and meat from Gregg. I made the bread, the house was free, I managed to belong to the London Library who sent us books – and there was also a wonderful second-hand bookshop in the town where we went occasionally with Gregg when he took us in his car.'

'Why did you stop the music?'

'It stopped itself. After your father's visit. He came to Wissingley to tell me he had run out of money and had to sell the house. When we moved to London, the music dried up. You can't just switch it on in your head.'

'What happened to your parents' house?'

'I don't know.'

'*What*?'

'You are shocked. But my last memories were standing in the churchyard in misty rain, thinking, "Can my parents really be in those two boxes . . . the earth open waiting to receive them and then close?" I stood outside *on* the earth, and knew I would never see them again. I kept going back and haunting the graveyard, thinking they must speak to me, that there would be a sign. And if *only* I could stay with Grandpa . . . I was terrified of the arrangement that had been made to send me away, but had no power to refuse. When the day of departure came I clung to the old man in panic. He seemed very sad also. How could he have guessed that the cousin's wife would hate me . . . So you see, what happened to the house after that was on another dimension.'

She looked at me with a sweet, gentle expression.

'Old Tim,' she said, 'Timmy dear, I am sorry. I did actually write, after I had grown up, and ask my cousin about it, from Wissingley. He answered to say that there had been large debts and he understood it had been sold at auction to pay them. And after my darling old grandpa was dead, all I wanted was to forget. Specially when our life at Wissingley was so wonderful . . .' She put her forehead into her hands then.

'We were happy,' she said, 'why disturb it?'

'Yes. But we haven't got Wissingley any more, that makes it different. Do you guess when I am thinking?'

'It's too late to check the accounts. I will write to the land register, to please you . . .'

'We should have had some money from it.'

'How worldly you have grown.'

'Will you write, just so that we know?'

'Yes. But don't hope. It has surely long gone. Maybe you should study law.'

'With no schooling?'

'*That* is not too late.'

'One more thing. What of my *Russian* grandfather?'

'Not Russian. My mother's father was a diplomat who lived a long time in Russia; he met Chekhov, he knew Diaghilev – when he retired he came to live with us. He taught me Russian songs . . . he was my beloved old *douchka*.'

I stood up feeling stiff in all my bones, and looked out of the window at the eternal feet walking in our street. I had found out about my family at last. My father sounded like a lunatic but I was excited to know I had Egyptian blood; I came from the place where the swallows go. Our room felt timeless now, Ma was quiet, and as I saw the parade of feet of the Londoners passing by outside I thought of the swallows. Each September Ashley and I used to watch them grouping for take-off –preening, twittering, assembling on the telephone wires – and then one morning there was an empty left-behind feeling with the sky bare, and we knew they had gone, that the summer was over and winter would creep up inevitably from then on; late summer had a tired feel. Riding to school we would calculate how long the swallows would take to get to Egypt. 'It's three days now, do you think they are there?' 'Do they come down to rest on the way?' It was drear at first after they had gone, until the robin sang. It was usually a few days later, one morning a robin would warble the way they do briefly in autumn – and he would seem pleased, as if he had regained his kingdom, the noisy summer visitors had gone. To him swallows were probably just jet-setter tourists who wanted summer all year round. After the robin took over, a new season started, his song was the beginning of the red and yellow colours when autumn would settle into place and the land would shine. Red berries, gaunt trees showing their design when the leaves had gone, cobwebs on the yew in the fog . . . bicycling to school as the mists lifted into sunlight . . . and once winter set in, talk by the fire on dark afternoons, cold outside and my mother reading aloud.

'Oh Timmy,' her voice said, sounding forlorn, and I was jolted back to London.

I had been hundreds of miles away, I was concentrating on being Egyptian, belonging to the far-away places where the swallows went. Luxor. James.

Camels? But I turned from the window and entered again our basement room, and knew that she was feeling bad partly because of having had to bring up her old memories. 'You'll feel better now,' I said, like somebody's nanny when a child has been sick. 'You can forget again.'

Wissingley had returned serenely for the first time since we had left it, and brought peace.

The letter box banged upstairs as something was thrown through it and landed on the floor in the hall; steps retreated into the street. The postman. A letter. Our life focused as it really was; I must hurry now to pass exams and make some money. We needed things; she even needed clothes. Everything was back in its usual place and I dreaded the telephone.

Ten

I was in the big shop when I saw the scarf. It was a silky veil of emerald green, many yards long. I loitered round the counter, wanting it for her, and started working out how to go about it. Why did Sam never bring anything? He just came to dinner and said (she told me) he liked our life because it was 'real', the way his life had been when he started. Does he know it's on real credit? One day he doesn't come and doesn't even bother to let her know. I am annoyed that my resentment has returned, as I had grown used to him. But since our dinner, though we had a specially good evening, I am angry again because she is fretting. There has been no news since. If he does come back maybe I'll go and live with Sally, I'm fed up with this plus-or-minus-Sam equation.

Once he did take her out to dinner. I remember she got dressed in some old shift type of black thing and tied a long red scarf round the waist, it looked fine. (Maybe that's why I liked the green scarf in the shop, it was her sort of thing.) They went to some 'unreal' place, I suppose I mean trendy and full of slobs, because next day there was a photograph of them in the evening paper, he must be a tycoon – and after that he always came to her. He didn't like publicity – or anyway being seen with Ma.

But lovers give presents (specially millionaires). It is sentimental and sexy and normal, ever since cavemen. I give Sally things, even if only whisky or little bunches from our garden. (I might as well get her a scarf too while I'm at it.) I wish Arthur would return to see us . . . but maybe he found us spooky, clipping jasmine in the moonlight, maybe on second thoughts – waking the next day – it had just been an outing. (Had my father ever given her anything? She said he was a miser. But also that he could be so nice – and was glamorous – and she had loved him in the beginning. Yet she seemed to have no rings . . .)

I went often to the shop to wander round and study the lay-out. It would be possible to take the scarf if I carried my raincoat over my arm and managed to get it caught in the folds of the coat as if I had been jostled and had not noticed, specially if this was on a Saturday when there would be crowds. I practised at home – but must not delay or the scarf would be sold. I saw Swan's point about stealing – that is, the way he first did it long ago when he still had some kind of values. My rule would be never to steal personal belongings. But a big shop was different; the owner was probably a miser like Sam and my dad. (I did not tell myself it might be the thin edge of the wedge. I thought it would only happen once – then I would get on with my exams and proper work for the future. I forgot that Swan had found it exciting and got hooked.)

The days continued to go by with no news of Sam. His failure to appear remained a mystery, I was beginning to have hope, though I jumped when the telephone rang. The best part was that now Ma fretted less, she was much more peaceful since our wild evening. Maybe telling her story had got rid of a lot of old bile and gave her a new start. If only James would happen to be in the street. (James was not mean, I remembered, he always brought things . . .)

Saturday came. The plan went off so easily I felt quite shaken . . . I got two scarves, the green one and another blue with a pattern . . . but walking back I did not feel the glorious victor I had expected to be, I felt guilty. It was a cheat; the presents weren't from me. I hadn't earned them, or had I, by risking myself?

When I got home she was washing the floor, a sight I particulary hated. I said, 'Get up, Ma, and go and clean up because I've got you something' – ordering her about like a man of fifty. She did as she was told, came back with her hair brushed and stood waiting, demure. I wrapped the long scarf round her twice and it hung down like some sort of dress, yet so fine it could fold small and go in a pocket.

'Oh,' she said, 'a sari,' in the specially quiet voice she used for Events. Then she felt it carefully, spreading it wide, holding it up. She looked at me in a funny way but didn't ask where it came from. Thank God she didn't say it must have been expensive, how could I afford it – I would have blushed scarlet. Anyway that sort of remark was not her style.

'Old Tim. Thank you. A present.' She folded it very carefully and laid it on top of the piano, glancing at it, then back at me. Did she guess? There was nothing more to say I suppose; I hoped she liked it, and thought she probably did because she had that light shining out of her eyes.

And then the telephone rang. His voice was so loud I could hear it across the room, 'It is I!' he shouted. What self-importance. 'I'm coming right over with vodka and caviar.' Well at least he was bringing something for the first time; this was her day for presents. But why should he come whenever it suited, why was she so easy to get, might she not be busy? 'There was a robbery at my house the other night,' his voice went on, 'that was why I could not come. I have been up to my ears in insurance papers and the police.'

I had a vision of his house in the country lined with precious stones, probably a gold mosaic swimming pool, and exotic Indian cranes strutting about eating caviar and belching out of snooty beaks, looking sideways at the guests.

'You might have let me know,' said my mother, and I thought: good for her.

'We'll have three courses of caviar to make up for it.'

'Well don't come yet – make it a bit later.' This was a slight improvement.

'Show him the scarf,' I said when she rang off. 'Let him be jealous. You don't know how to handle men.'

'I don't want to *handle* anyone,' she said.

I left the house and unexpectedly threw up in the street. Was it shame with myself for stealing, and fear, and then having the nerve to preach to other people?

I went to see Sally, wanting her as a friend to talk with and to bring her the news that I had Egyptian blood! To laugh together. Perhaps I was looking for some sort of comfort underneath, I don't know, but the atmosphere was not what I had expected and we argued. It came back to Sam again; she gave me a lecture saying I should stop feeling involved. I said, 'If you lived in the same house *you*'d feel involved, it's obsessive.'

'Your mother needs to love,' Sally said. 'Let her have him and be happy. Love for a cad is an old story, there's even a sort of beauty in it.'

'Except that she isn't happy.'

She said crossly that I didn't understand about love. I hadn't come there to discuss love, I dislike scenes, so I went away, very disappointed. And I had forgotten to bring the other scarf . . . I had been intending to come saying: I am an Egyptian!! A new man! And here is a present! It was a flop.

It was late when I got home after some night rambling, having reverted to my 'walking-cure'. My mother's door was closed – he must be there.

I paced about in the basement pondering on Sally's wisdom, trying to be glad Ma had this man, trying to see it as a wonderful Godsend, trying also to think: what do I care anyway? I stood at the window looking out at the early-morning emptiness – 2.30 a.m. – the swish of a taxi with plumes of wet behind it – a couple walking . . .

I heard them go downstairs to the hall and then saw them standing on the front steps – in complete silence; it had a final quality. He said, 'Why do you regret me? I can't afford these feelings, it will mess my life. I just wanted you, not love.'

'You love me then?' she asked.

'Yes.'

'So you want safety.'

'Despise me, it will make it easier.'

He took her hand rather formally and kissed it. 'You'll find a much better man,' he said.

'I have nothing to give another man.'

I couldn't believe it. He was leaving her. After all my prayers for this thing to end – then being convinced by Sally than on the contrary it should continue for ever and 'let her be happy' . . . at least if it ended *she* should be the one to take leave, with no pangs, it shouldn't be this way, so she would suffer. How did he dare?

He went down the steps and got into his car. She was standing in the doorway; she must have looked dreadful because he said, 'I don't want that face. Please wave me off smiling . . . My best girl I ever had . . .' (How common, I thought.) Then he started the engine and his long barracuda car began sliding very slowly out of the picture, like his fleet of ships or whatever his money come from – leaving no trace on the sea. There is an Arab proverb: three things leave no mark, a stone in water, a snake in grass, a man in woman. She was just standing there in her nightdress, on the steps where I had vomited earlier.

In a flash I was out of the door and down the street after him. I caught up with his car, he was cruising quietly, as if he was going over something in his mind. I banged on the door. 'Stop!' I shouted.

He slowed further but did not quite stop. '*Please!*' I was yelling so loud that some lights went on in the house opposite. He stopped then and opened the window. 'What do you want?' he asked coldly.

'I want to talk to you man to man.' I had my hand inside the window and was pushing the door handle: in thirty seconds I had had a revelation, an about-face on all my former opinions.

'Are you sure you're really her son?' he asked, sarcastic.

'You think I've got a mother fixation, but you don't understand – she has no husband or brother or father – only me to care about her . . .'

Another light had gone on in a second house; I had been shouting, windows were opening, I knew he hated publicity and scandal, I had not been yelling on purpose though, there seemed to be an outside force directing me. He got out of his car – my hands closed round his throat – but when he choked I let go – *What on earth was I doing*? I felt frantic and quite mad . . .

here I was begging and dragging him back when all I had ever wanted was his end . . . my head would burst with thinking about this bloody man – but, whatever happened it should not be *this* – he should not be marching off like King Solomon.

We went back into the house together; my mother was sitting in the hall. He laid his hand on her cheek for a moment; he was showing tenderness – but she paid no attention and seemed dazed – as I felt too . . . What was real, the cad, or the domestic man? And now that he was here, what in the devil's name did I want to say? We were face to face for the first time since the hold-up, that night of kid's stuff that seemed so long ago. I had never spoken more than one sentence to him; now we looked at each other straight. He seemed to scrutinize me for a long time, looking back at my mother, then again at me.

'Poor old fellow,' he said finally, after much thought, and he smiled and slapped my arm; not patted, slapped like equals. He had a slight accent which I had not noticed before, he was foreign. In the timeless night-dawn between two days, the draw-bridge was down.

'You're quite a boy,' he said. 'I was wrong about you. You should indeed protect her. But what is it you want?'

'Christ,' I said, blushing and chaotic inside. 'I knew it clearly but I don't now. You aren't like I thought, either.'

'You didn't like me, and why should you? It's what I stand for.'

'Can't you give her something?'

'If she needs anyting, she has only to ask me.'

'She would never ask. And I don't mean that sort of thing, necessarily. Something ordinary like a walk in the park – a telephone number where she could ring you if she wants to talk, not just wait and wonder . . . something human, or something bigger, go away on a trip . . . You cheat my mother and you cheat your wife – so in the end you also cheat yourself . . . I know it's none of my business, and yet it *is*. You have taken over the house.' I was breathless. It didn't sound right, it wasn't entirely what I meant, and its great importance had vanished.

'Son,' he said (this sounded dramatic and I felt near tears), 'I didn't mean it to be this way.'

In the first daylight that was slowly establishing itself, he looked tired and seemed older, like some Mediterranean papa, like Raimu in the movie I had seen with James.

'She was a windfall – it was just a lark, but the lark sang. I decided it should not go on, it was getting out of hand. But we have been happy, or had until now. Neither of us wanted to go away on a trip as you suggest; her little room contained our world. But I have a wife I married twenty years ago, and two sons. I'm not a cheat on purpose. Life makes you cheat; have you never done so?

I turned scarlet.

'I work hard,' he said. 'To take time to walk in the park is not easy . . .' and he laughed as if the idea amused him. 'Would you want me to leave my family?'

'Do they bore you?'

'Yes – well – it's routine.'

'Why should marriage be prison?' I cried. 'What is

wrong with the world and its rules? Maybe your wife is bored too – why not let each other fly?'

'That will be your generation,' he said. 'To invent a new arrangement. We are set in our ways, my old wife cannot fly. I don't know what to do about it, so I thought it right not to go on doing *this*.'

All this time Ma was sitting quiet, appearing fatalistic, to be in her own cloud as if she had nothing to do with us; she was being rather creepy, I thought. I looked back again at him and noticed there was a mark on his throat where I had grabbed him in the street. I had hated him with the stupidity of Duddo for so long – and he had called me son . . . With a sort of despair I wanted to belong, to be a family, like his wife and sons. I longed for a father I never knew I missed.

He talked. He told me he was Greek and had lived on an island till he was twelve – nobody went to his island, even now. He had come to England, owning nothing, when he was fifteen. He was one of those legends – wore no shoes as a child – and I was meeting one of the people I had read about in so many newspapers, whose story was almost too classic to believe, yet he was there in front of me, a true person. If he and Ma could only have met before . . . and if I had not always behaved like a Victorian grandfather – perhaps living with only one parent a fellow doesn't have a chance – (Swan said I 'talked grown-up', he said I was a pain) – and now I felt crazy and inside-out, I wanted to be his son, I wanted to roll on the floor and yell, I didn't know what the hell any more, everything familiar was breaking up . . . but I was happy . . . I was on the highest cloud ever.

'I'm sorry Sam,' I said, 'I've behaved like a fool.' Trying to be dignified and hold on to my manhood. 'But please don't leave her like she is now, she's gone all peculiar. Could you stay here, just for tonight, could you wait till morning?'

'It *is* morning,' he said, and I saw him in full daylight, our great new day just beginning, for something new must surely come out of this. He took Ma's arm and they went upstairs.

I went to my room but could not possibly sleep, nor did I try to. A great change had come into our life. What would happen now. Would he maybe divorce? He did not need to abandon his family, they would have his name and money . . . If they were bored together, as he said, it would not hurt anyone. Perhaps he could give me a job – I could work at something properly. If he had started out himself with no shoes he would understand my limitations and take me on with no qualifications. I began to pace my room and make plans, imagining myself to be a normal son in a normal family, unaware that I was being ridiculous.

Daylight arrived completely and sunlight came into the room; birds sang in the gardens behind the houses, I heard the milkman. I was glowing, telling myself: I knew that some day we'd got to win . . . and I went downstairs to start to prepare them a succulent first breakfast together, the beginning of domesticity: the sort of strong black coffee a Greek would like, bacon and eggs – I cut the bread ready for the toast and laid the table.

She came down alone at eight o'clock; I jumped up to hug her – but stopped. What was it?

'He's dead,' she said.

Eleven

It was the last thing I remember her saying to me: 'He's dead.' We must have spoken in the next few days, but I don't recall the content, only that if I had shot him with a gun her feeling for me could not have been clearer. Perhaps it was true, I had wanted him dead for so long with such concentration – until the last night – that perhaps I had killed him. And how could she know I had changed – that I had fallen for him too?

'You – cope please,' her voice said.

In the sickening morning seen as in a room in some other person's life in some other town, another person's hand (only it was mine) picked up the telephone and called the police. The things that followed were like news photographs, only they were happening to us. The body under the sheet and the questions. The doctor coming. He said it was a heart attack and happened all the time, specially to high-powered businessmen who worked too hard, then he said he was in a hurry and went on to the next patient.

There was an inquest. It was peculiar the way he died, they said, and what were those marks on his throat? The wife came into court and shrieked abuse at my mother. I stared from my seat and was not a man any more, I was a small boy who cried. I terribly wanted someone, or some faith, something to hold. Or Gregg, Jake, James . . . oh bring him back. Make it not true . . . My body could not contain this day, this courtroom, it would crack and my heart would fall out and be burnt with the rubbish from Sam's last dinner. The street was full of dustmen when we left the building, his dinner remains were still in our bin; it was impossible he would not come back . . . The Thing under the cover could not be him? No longer a person, so motionless, so rigid and cold . . .

We appeared in court twice. The wife (too old to fly) kept screaming, 'The harlot, the bitch,' pointing at my mother. Ma sat looking small and distant with her mane of hair matted and unbrushed. She did not defend herself, she had nothing to say. I was furious at the abuse and the false image of her they presented. (Didn't they know she soothed the nerves of poor Mrs Gregg, she could talk to dangerous horses, she was kind?) She just sits there and doesn't answer.

The judge asked me if we had ever received anything from Sam. Yes I said, trouble, Sam and this redshanker city had brought trouble. He asked if my mother had received money or presents. I said, never, not a flower, he didn't give, he took, he even took her from me. I did not mean to load Sam, since at the last it had all changed, but now I couldn't stand the sight of his wife, and was angry with the suspicion of the judge, and anyway he *had* brought trouble – if he didn't take some responsibility for it the alternative was for them to blame my mother. She needed protection. But she only spoke in monosyllables.

The wife kept screeching, 'She killed my husband!' The doctor said he was due for a heart attack and would have had one anyway sooner or later, 'death was only timing'. I looked at Ma, hoping she had heard that, since it would relieve the pressure from me – had she *heard* that it only *happened* to occur in our house? but she might have been deaf for all the sign she gave. Why were the legal men so suspicious of us, what had we gained from any of this?

They asked me if I had wished Sam dead, and I said yes many times, because it had been true. The junior counsel said it was the wrong thing to say. I said I had changed my views about him before he died. Had I wished him dead when we met in the street? Were the marks on the throat made by me? I said yes, but the doctor said he did not die of them, the death was natural, and the wife repeated that he died of the shock we had caused. Case dismissed.

When it was over, and since my mother seemed to dislike the sight of me, I went to live with Sally – but our love was spoiled too, because discussions about Sam led to bitter arguments. These grew to such a size I could not study or work, I did not know what to do and started stealing again in order to buy whisky and food, I did not want Sally to keep me on her teacher's pay and what did my resolutions matter now? Indeed Sam had indirectly brought us doom, my old premonitions were true. I kept thinking of the wife shrieking because she was legally married, virtuous, wronged. What of the wrong she did Sam by being a bore? That did not count in court, it was not a misdemeanour. She could not have been jealous of Sam any more – or does jealousy last for ever? Was it not more to do with pride, freedom and Ma living outside convention? I hated the judges and the people who made the rules.

I did not see my mother after the trial. Sally said she was in shock and would need me later. I kept telling Sally (who did not understand and, for the first time, seemed to me dense) that my mother couldn't face me because I was involved.

'You should go to her,' Sally would say. 'She brought you up, taught you to read, to dive through the waves . . .'

'She thinks I killed her lover who made the best waves.' But Sally went on trying to rid me of this feeling, and I was irritated by her inability to see for herself what she had told me so often before, that it really had been a love affair and not just infatuation – so the sadness would last for ever . . .

We were continually at cross-purposes. I started to withdraw from her, she looked at this tragedy the wrong way, like people who stare at road accidents, though I knew she was trying to help – yet she clipped out the newspaper reports and kept them in her scrapbook . . . I found it hard to control my temper. The obsession I could not get rid of was that if I had not interfered, Sam's death would not have happened in our house.

'But since he had it coming, he would be dead anyway,' Sally would repeat – and I would answer again and again, 'Can't you see that Ma would have accepted it if it had been somewhere else? But she thinks I brought it on. Her son. Not fate, fire or flood. *Me.*'

'Nonsense,' cried Sally, flushed, 'she would have been deprived of him anyway. It's the *same void*, no matter what causes the deprivation.'

'How do you know?'

'Because that is how it will be when you've gone! And the more I know it, the more I annoy you and chase you away! I can't help it. And after you've gone, I'll have the void.'

I stared at her; I had had no idea.

'*Me*?' I was staggered. 'But I'm a kid you've passed the time with. Literature lessons. You're twelve years older, you can have real men.'

'Exactly,' wept Sally, 'I'm twelve years older and there's the horror of it. You are a real man for me, but I would not put you in a net, even if some women are twelve years older than their husbands - oh I've thought about it, but I would be frightened - and those marriages usually take place in middle age when people have lived first - a man of thirty might marry a woman of forty-two, but . . .'

I was dumbfounded, it was my turn to be dense. She had circles under her eyes. She must have been sleepless and crying . . . how could I have guessed . . . But for me, our affair had died with Sam because of our arguments - or some other outside factor - the current had been cut. She was a schoolteacher aged twenty-nine. She was poor Sally. I was sorry for her but pity is the death of desire.

★

They caught me stealing, so it solved the problem of where I should live. I was not careful, they must have been watching me since the inquest.

When I said goodbye to Sally she said, 'Your mother will need you later.'

'I'll be in the borstal if she wants my address,' I said, angry with them both.

'Don't forget me completely,' she said. 'One day when you're forty, think: Sally loved me.'

It was terrible. She looked terrible. How many years had she been twenty-nine? It was a mean thought, but a person can't help their thoughts. Our magnificent thing had gone dead. It was inexplicable, beyond understanding, but it had happened.

The last time I saw her I went down the stairs (where the old man opened his door looking through the crack, letting out a smell of cabbage, as he did each time anyone passed) and I did not look back, though I could feel her standing in the doorway waiting for me to wave. I was alone for the rest of my life, hated by my mother, and feeling that waving makes things worse. I have never seen her since. I let her down, but could not help it.

Twelve

They sent me to the Youth Custody Centre where Swan had done his time. It must have been taken into account that I was his friend, and under suspicion of drug peddling with him, because otherwise a first offence (and mine was only for shoplifting) does not warrant prison. A pusher would get gaol, a junkie who just takes it himself would not. I was neither, so what had Swan told them? How would it help him to implicate me? He had been my friend once . . . was this some revenge on Mr Right? Or was he so high that he did not know what he was saying . . . the night we had been together, it was he who had pointed me out to the police . . .

When I was interviewed they said my mother was absent from her address and asked if I knew where she might be. We are out of touch, I told them. The case with Sam was brought up again, the 'unexplained marks' on his throat were mentioned. I made no comment. 'What is this murky, self-contained boy?' I heard one of them say. 'What aberration has he? Is he too old to be in Care?' Care!! Inwardly I howled. Care in someone's home! 'What class does he come from?' came next. Class, their obsession. My mother was outside class, therefore so was I. She is an artist, I wanted to say, a musician; or earthy, a peasant preferably, with green fingers for vegetables. Or an intellectual who reads. My father was half Egyptian, we would not fit any of their labels. Middle-class, working-class, East End boy . . . settled everything for them. Once a fellow could be fitted into their pattern he would conform to their ideas and no longer be himself.

My hearing in the juvenile court seemed to me biased, but perhaps by Swan's information, not by them. Only a first offence, yet I was being sent Inside; the Sam-skirmish must have made it worse. I pleaded guilty to stealing only. (And how else to get by in a consumer society? I might do it again, though I disapproved.) 'My ancestors were Pharaohs,' I told the court. Odd boy, they nodded at each other. The verdict was one year.

The prison was somewhere in Kent, it took two hours to get there, and when the coach reached the big gates I saw 'Borstal Institute 1908' written in bricks. The end of a future. But I liked the name better than Youth Custody Centre, which was genteel and a pretence. A spade is a spade and the prison gates are double – there is a space between them where the van waits, to make sure no one can get away while the first gate is being locked. Then – I was truly Inside, specially when from my building there was a window on the upper floor that looked over a high wall, and I could see Outside beyond, and smoke from chimneys of homes where other people were free to come and go. I had dreaded the possibility of seeing

Swan, fortunately he was not there.

It was not unlike school, except that it was never time to go home. The boys there are older, their ages from seventeen to twenty-one, and all over again it was fuck, piss and shit. At least I knew the difference between a Rachel and a Sally. Perhaps they did, but certainly they did not show it, they spoke of having girls like any bodily function, there was never anything lovely about it, and yet in their cells they had pictures of them - usually leaning over, seen from behind and wearing black suspenders, and with their breasts hanging down. So perhaps their language was just a front. The black suspenders seemed stereotyped to me, but that was probably my grandpa side. They had sensual feeling, but no emotion, but then I was like that before I met Sally. I felt a physical revulsion from them because of their smell . . . and then gradually, I grew sorry for them. Without exception they came from loveless homes in cities. I had been lucky, even if the love I had had was an eiderdown. I tried to join them and belong in their group, listening to their plans to steal again as soon as they got out, but it did not work - I did not really want stealing as a way of life for the future. In time, I discovered that they were not a group either in spite of their similar ambitions, there were no friendships between them. They were all loners, yet they understood each other, that was the difference and their resentment of me, I was another sort of animal. I saw no way ahead now, all I wanted was to get back to the land and black out.

They had visitors. By request and arrangement they were permitted to go to Visitors' Hall where they could sit at a table and talk, usually to a friend their age. I noticed that few families came. But some people Outside cared. No one came to see me. I couldn't figure out about Ma. I would have welcomed Rachel (who must be permanently stoned now) or any girl I had known – someone to talk to . . . and to bring me sweets. We were hooked on sweets; no alcohol was allowed, so sweets made up for it. Visions of sherbet, strawberries and toffee crunch filled our thoughts; there was a shop where Mars bars and chocolates were obtainable, but our allowance was only £2 a week, which did not go far. We earned this by work: cleaning the hallway, washing the floor, scrubbing the lavatories, kitchen duty. Sex was another obsession, usually somehow foul. There were training courses: home decorating, motor mechanics, making bricks. I liked being assigned to the garden, so-called – it consisted of clipping hedges and mowing grass – because this duty was outside the wall and done under surveillance. One boy spent his entire allowance on Johnson's oil for his skin.

Our cells contained a bed, a table and chair and a chamber pot. One boy had a pin-up of a car, or half a car since the wheels were missing, which he gazed at in rapture. Another had made his own drawing of a woman in a rocking chair with a potted plant and a cat. I decided he must have had a decent home, but he never spoke to me so I never found out. The others all had naked girls, or the ones in underclothes. I had nothing on my wall. They couldn't figure this: don't you want something to look at? My blank was like a crystal ball where I saw different things at different times - usually land, or a foreign city with James.

Occasionally the Governor came to see us and made some brief conversation; it aroused in me a desire to talk, but I had no pretext to ask for an interview, which would be granted for a purpose like permission to receive a friend, not just for chat. I wondered how this man had started his career. He was as enclosed as we were in his fashion - though he could go home at night, we were his world and he spent most of his life Inside. Did he believe in redemption? What sort of job would be open to us when we got out, yobbos with a record - would we not be the last to find work, with unemployment so rife? I wished we could discuss this with him. One morning at breakfast I remarked that I liked him, and was jeered at. I called them ostracizers. 'What does that mean? We want no asshole swells here giving us bullshit.' Yet when the Governor was there they called him Sir as if filled with genuine respect, meek and cowed.

We had television and a games room; we watched American movies when possible, or crime and detective serials, or sport. They did not care about news or what happened to the world. Life settled into a familiar monotony, until one day there was a murder.

A pair of scissors had been overlooked after the

decorating course on wallpaper hanging (we were not allowed to possess scissors or knives); two boys had a fight that developed into a brawl, one of them grabbed the scissors and plunged them into the other one's chest - but at random, he did not aim, it happened in rage. The stabbed boy collapsed with blood spouting from his mouth and was carried away. A lung had been pierced, the scissors had entered at a fatal place. He died later.

The shock united us into a brief brotherhood. There were no hardened criminals among us, we were petty thieves, guilty at worst of house-breaking, bodily violence and assault. For a time we 'all stood together' like the Paul McCartney song. The wretch who committed the murder was given a life sentence and transferred, we never saw him again, but I brooded about him. It had been unintentional - as a result his own life was over, even when sentence was reduced to manslaughter. The act had been ghastly to see, I was haunted, and also felt pity. But our brotherhood lasted only twenty-four hours, then the sparring resumed.

On afternoons when there was no gymnasium or work course we were banged up, closed into our cells. There was nothingness. At three o'clock there was a break for a wash and the lavatories - we trailed out with our sponge bags - then back. Lie there. Imagine something. Read - but read what? In one building there was a bookcase known as the library, this produced detective books and porn. I learned from the guard that requests for special books were allowed, though there were no requests. But it meant I could ask for a book . . . So where to start? I realized I had read what I found in the shelves at home, or under direction of Sally or Ma. In order to decide, I would like to browse in a library. Perhaps I could learn a language while I was here, I could ask for a Spanish grammar . . . then get a job in Spain, on a ranch . . .? Nothing came of this, I sank into lethargy and stared at my blank wall through the eternal afternoons when we were banged up. Sometimes I would see Swan's face, or an imagined village in Greece where Sam came from and where James went. James helped me through prison, as I kept imagining the things he had told me. On his first visit to Morocco he had expected exotic women in veils, but had seen them swathed in coarse sheets, trudging the streets in galumphy shoes – he told me about a village in Austria where he went to ski, and the accordion music in the evenings with men dancing in leather shorts and *edelweiss* on their hats – he gave me a vision of Europe that wasn't just England . . . and then the view would be blocked by Ma. How could she leave me here with no news? I alternated between grief and anger. Could she really not care? Why did she not come to see me? Then I would be cross. *What the hell.* And see Sam's body again, Sam dead. She had talked of acceptance of her parents' death. Had she accepted Sam now? *I miss you, Ma.*

The guard said, 'You're lucky. In Wormwood Scrubs

the fellows are banged up for twenty-three hours a day.'

'You mean they only have *one hour* out?'

'Yes. They can run around the yard for one hour. That's all.'

So we were lucky. And because of all the time I spent in greyness, I started writing an account of my life, of what happened – it became an occupation. It is meant for a judge to read. Please, Your Honour, there is something wrong with the way people are judged. I don't really know what I am guilty of, it seems much worse than what I did. Please judge Ma kindly if she comes back in court – I feel the case is not over, and that is why maybe she has left town – otherwise would she not come to see me? She brought me up for a world that doesn't exist, or not any more. My father took our home away when I was eight, a person can break out later according to what happens then. The boys in here all come from tower blocks, they had no space outside – their parents seem to ignore them. One of them told me that only five people in his whole building had jobs. So what are they supposed to do? And does anyone care what happens to them?

As I lay in my cell thinking and writing, our house above the grocer's shop seemed like a palace in my memory. And I kept wondering if Ma's hair was still black by candlelight or if the shock had turned it white. Was she growing old? There was no provision for her old age, and it must be creeping up on her now like the tide in the creek below Wissingley. I would close my eyes and remember the squelching noise of water round the rushes and reeds . . . But in a way Ma felt dead. Sometimes in my writing she was Ma with a capital letter, at others just ma like a table or chair. She must be dead or she would come to see me. Maybe she just lay in bed and didn't eat. There is too much time to think, in a cell. What would have happened if Sam had lived? I would not be in here, to start with. Great love must end in tragedy, they say. Then is it better to belong to the ninety per cent who don't have it? Not to know is better than to live with loss for the rest of time?

I tried not to think of Sally (your hair is like silk; your face is lined but I don't mind), but I wrote her a letter once. (Please forgive me, I didn't wave.) I tore it up. She told me I was a dinosaur, the boys here think I am a freak . . . Has Ashley got his scholarship . . .? Please let Swan not be sent here . . .

There was a chapel with Church of England services on Sundays, some boys attended as an occupation. I liked listening to the sermons, it gave me something to think about. Out of the three hundred and fifty of us, sixty went to church, I used to count them. A Catholic priest came to visit once a month, also a rabbi. One day some divinity students came; I wanted to ask them questions but could not find the words. In the endlessness of these days, all I could really do was go back over the past, because there was no present. And always, there would be that empty hole. Did she still visit the old ladies, holding out her home-made cake like a banner? Or has she volunteered to work in a leper colony? The day I left our house, the grocer's shop was in the process of being sold, our flat above it included, but the grocer said the lease could be renewed if she wanted it. So what had happened?

Always I looked anxiously at the new faces of boys arriving, checking that Swan was not among them. I hoped never to see him again, though he was my first city friend. He and Ashley were the only ones I ever had.

A year passed and one day it was over; when this truly happened it was a shock. I had grown used to living without beginning or end, and - unexpectedly - to go out into the free world again felt unsafe. We had been protected. The coach that drove five of us back to London was an ordinary bus, so the people in the street didn't know where we came from; we should already be feeling like normal human beings, with no shame. Yet I was scared, and the other boys also seemed subdued. There was no feeling of excitement, rather of apprehension. We did not like each other, so there was no talk or comparing of thoughts. We arrived - and dispersed - going our different ways.

There I stood, in a street where I was free to walk; but I didn't know where to go. If someone spoke to me, what would I say? I had been given the address of a probation officer, but did not feel inclined to see him. There would be a well-meaning lecture and I would wonder if he believed what he was saying. There were agencies where I could apply for a job -

but I would just be put on a list and then directed to a hostel where I would have to sleep with other young men, all outsiders as usual.

I got a train and then a bus with the money I had been given, and when it ran out I hitch-hiked back to the land I knew, and when the last ride ran out, I walked. When I got into the countryside, at last, I felt free.

Thirteen

So now I am at Wissingley, except that there is no house – I stand and look round me in a clearing where the land is ragged; there are old logs piled high, their trees must have been felled long ago because they are grown over with fungus and moss. White clematis beards shroud the hedges, interwoven with yellow bindweed and nettles. (She called him Nettlebed.) This is where the house used to be. I remember, remember and feel peculiar.

I went to the village, walking the five-mile road, a foreigner. Nobody knew me, but I knew their church and their pub. Where is the old thatched post office though, is it that new brick building?

It was not the same postmaster, but he chatted amiably. He told me they were going to build an estate on the Wissingley land, which explained why they had bulldozed the house. So then why had nothing been done in all this time? Because of permits, the green belt, and arguments about where the new road would be. New road? Possibly a dual carriageway. They could not agree on its course, he said.

I am on my own new road again because this place is finished; there are pylons, and bungalows along what used to be Featherbed Lane; they are taming it and giving it a suburban heart. One should never go back, I should never have come here, just kept it as an old dream . . . yet I *had to*, I was drawn. But it's over now.

My favourite programme on television in the borstal was the sheepdog trials; I always liked the look of Northumberland. Maybe I'll go north (but not to Yorkshire, that is Sally's place). I am eighteen with no O-levels or A-levels but I have read a lot, though that is probably of no use. I could be a farmhand. I might find a job in the country . . . If I could find a place for her too maybe her music would return. I started to hum the descant she wrote for 'Johnny's so Long at the Fair' . . . it had weird minor chords. In the song Johnny never came back.

Do your own thing, people say. Only she has to be all right and not ashamed; I owe her something. It was on this same road all those years ago that I asked her if we had nothing of our own, and she said, 'I've got you,' and I remember the breakers rolling up the shore with the hollow sound of rasping shingle stones, the noise carried because there was a west wind; it was nearly always a west wind, coming straight across the ocean from America, and when there was a storm it sounded fearsomely loud. The breakers are still the same because no one can tame the sea; the beach is still wild with a treacherous undertow at outgoing tide; the postmaster told me the National Trust has bought the headland.

'We did not die with Sam because I refuse to think that way,' I said (as I talked to her inside), 'though for a while we both went numb, but I kept saying what you taught me: don't sit down under it, don't accept.' Perhaps I could get a job looking after horses . . . *breaking in* horses must be well paid. Would a racehorse stable hire me? I can save money and buy a cottage no Visitor can come and claim. Maybe I should go and see Gregg . . .

Gregg. At this thought I stopped. I had been shy of seeing him, unable to face him after so much murky water under the bridge . . . yet truly I could not return here, and then leave again forever without seeing him . . . though I wished it could have been after I had found a job, not as a failure. But since I was never coming back . . .

I turned and started off again in the other direction. He lived seven miles out of the village, two miles beyond our house or four by the road. I knew the way across the moors; when I was six, I once dared myself to walk it in the moonlight alone. The shadows of the gorse bushes had looked like witches crouching, the excitement had been goose-flesh. His farm had belonged originally to Wissingley, but luckily he had bought it in time, and all this land I was crossing now was his - and as I walked and climbed, I saw that the higher I got up the hill, the more it started to look the same as before; gradually, going up the sheep track through the heather and peat, the realization came: the pylons and new roads don't show from here.

I sat on the gate that enclosed his fields from the small lane that led to his farmhouse, and puzzled. What should I say to him? And what will *he* say? How are you? Fine, I've been Inside, I learned to steal in the city, though I didn't really mean to, which makes it worse, it shows I am weak, - and my mother was called names in court - a man died in strange circumstances in our house, there was an inquest. He admired my mother, why burden him? Yet, after ten years, how could I not tell him anything? And what has Ashley become? He must be what my mother wanted me to be and here I am, a streetwise yob. And what of Jake? He must be at least fifteen - or dead. Maybe I couldn't bear to see him and have to leave him once more . . . So I turned again, zigzag thoughts, zigzag steps, and went back down the lane the other way. Ten years was too long to return with bad news. If I could have arrived in a car, brought presents . . . otherwise, better never to know. How long do cats live? What of our animals? Contradictions crossed and recrossed each other and confused me. Never go back. Keep to the north; follow the compass in your mind, not the one in your stomach. How far was Northumberland? I had no money. I felt dizzy.

A herd of ewes and a ram were approaching and behind them a young boy with a black-and-white Welsh sheepdog. He looked faintly familiar, could it be Gregg's son, Jamey? Who else on these uplands? When we went away I was eight and he was only four,

I never had much to do with him; now he would be fourteen. He nodded as he passed – and my resolution broke.

'Are you Jamey Gregg?' I asked.

He stopped in slight surprise.

'We used to live here – in that house that was pulled down.'

He had carrot-red hair like his father. He looked at me with a very slow smile.

'So you were those people,' he said. 'My father talks often of your mother, about how she helped with my mum, how she could dress wounded animals without their minding. You must be Timothy.'

Tim, the borstal kid, I thought.

'You're going the wrong way, if you're going to the farm,' he said.

'I have been for ten years.' (Never mind the cliché, it was true.)

'Come and see Dad.'

'All right, only call me Tim . . .'

We went. Following the sheep together with his dog, I felt myself falling into old habits, doing accustomed things. There were plover dipping and swerving overhead, with their small high cries, and a flock of redshank flying in close formation as they always did. *Redshank*! I had forgotten . . . it was so long since I had seen any . . . I had misjudged them and labelled them wrong.

★

Gregg was heavier, but with the same red-veined face that clashed with his hair, laughing and then cursing in strong language – it was his way. We sat at the kitchen table, Gregg, Jamey, a boy they called Herb and a silent older man – and we drank home-made beer, which tastes nothing like beer in pubs. I asked where his wife was and he said they took her to the asylum. To my horror I broke down and cried. I don't know why, I never liked the old bag – but something inside me snapped. Finally I told Gregg everything, and I had misjudged him – he had a countryman's acceptance of whatever happened as a natural disaster or bad season. He just said, 'What did you expect of town? Why don't you stay here? I need help. None of my men stay, I *really* need it.'

'I've got a record, anyone employing me should know. I've been a thief.'

'So are all the hired men here,' he said, grinning at Herb. 'Aw, you just went through a spell.' The older man kept his silence, but his eyes were piercing.

'They said in court that mother was a man-stealer, that she was no good, made out she was a gold-digger, yet she never even received a present.'

At this he turned purple as blueberries (whorts, they were called locally) and he shouted, 'I'll smash whoever said that!'

'A woman said it. You can't hit a woman.'

Then he laughed. 'A ninny I reckon. Must have lost her man. And what's wrong with another woman wanting her man if she can't please him? It's not against the law, nor Nature. We'll fetch her back and she can live here. I've got a big farm and need help, hear? But I'm not selling land, we'll manage better if there's more of us. I'll give you a good job, Timmy, an overseer you'll become.'

It was unreal – a tidy, happy ending like a movie. I felt stricken, as if none of this could be true. I didn't answer, but asked, 'What happened to Nero?'

'Broke his leg and had to be shot, kept galloping off, pounding all the turf, never had a rider who could cope.'

'Duddo?'

'Fought with my dogs, had to give him away. He changed character once he was here, he grew mean.'

Poor old fellow, I thought, he must have missed us. Then I saw, sitting on the dresser across the kitchen, an old, triangular, lean cat's face scrutinizing me. He knew me, or why did he stare? But why had he not approached? I called his name in the special voice I always used when he was far away – 'Jakey? Here Jakerakeraker . . .' and at that he jumped down on to the floor, walking with his tail up towards me; I picked him up and squeezed him hard. Gregg said he never let people hold him. In his cat's memory, somewhere in that small head, in his heart under the fur, he knew.

I started to believe. These are my people, my animals. Even Herb, who is new. And that silent-man who is now smiling. Suddenly I shouted, 'All right – I agree – you're on! I'll go and get her and we'll be back. Give me enough for the fare, an advance on my job.'

'I'll drive you to the station.'

'No, thanks, you did that last time. Besides, I couldn't sit still. I'll walk it. I'll run' – and I was away.

★

Now I'm running, but not from it, to it – flying along with the west wind pushing behind, across the hills and down to the end of the lane to get to the road, then the larger roads, the station, the train, back to the sooty city for the last time; I will find her at the second address the prison Governor gave me but where I couldn't face going at the time – and she'll live here, she'll sing on horseback again, she'll cook delicious meals and look after the men, maybe she'll warm someone's bed, it doesn't matter how it all happens – she is needed and that is the beginning; here is our first real start.

I'm passing the gate that opens on to the fields, some grouse have just whirred up out of the heather. Each squelch, each scrape of bramble tearing my jeans seems indented into me like a permanent tattoo. I'll put up with the new post office, I'll accept the pylons that don't show from here anyway, I'll get to know the new grocer . . . Gregg has six hundred acres of plover and partridge and sheep and juniper and whortleberry and *redshank* and farm land. And below the cliffs – the sea. We'll dive through the rollers again, I'll teach Jamey.

In the late-autumn sun I'm crying and laughing and sweating as I run fast to get to the train, clothes drenched, heart thudding, tall grass soggy, foot caught in bracken, fall down and get up again and keep running, running, turned inside out and shouting in the wind, my voice tearing and spiralling away, something has to explode. This familiar place looks new, it never looked so beautiful, my land, our land and her November – and I'm going to bring her back.

Fourteen

After a night spent in a station waiting room and then a long train journey, my spirits had somewhat subsided - and so on leaving Euston I decided to walk. It would give me time to ponder, before reaching my mother. I was eager still, but also apprehensive. What (who) would I find? I knew nothing of what had been happening to her, and it only occurred to me now that she might have changed. Before returning to Wissingley I had not even known whether I wanted to see her - but once there, in Gregg's world, a revelation had opened. Now - here was smelly old London again and a grey sort of different truth. The focus can change with the surroundings. Which one was real? However, I walked with long steps, proud and pleased, for I had at least now found *myself*. I was not afraid any more to speak to a person in the street, to ask the way or look them in the eye and smile, for I was a man with a job, I belonged and had a right to be there; Gregg's advance money had changed my whole being.

She lived in a block of flats overlooking a square with plane trees. As I reached the door, there she was walking out into the street. This was a shock and a come-down – I had imagined our reunion in the shadows, not harsh daylight. How much imagination had gone into my various mental pictures of this meeting and how it would take place . . . it was now sudden and ordinary. 'Oh,' we both said simultaneously – and then blushed, fidgeted and stared.

'Old Tim – it's about time,' she said.

'Christ, Ma,' I said, 'you have got a nerve.'

Then we both laughed, the tension ceased, but I still said, too polite, 'You were going somewhere . . . are you busy . . .?' and at that she cried, 'Don't be ridiculous. Come on in, stranger,' and the starch melted and I remembered, 'Come on in, tramp,' on the night of our no-Sam dinner, a hundred years ago.

She had two rooms with a door opening on to a modern, white kitchen – it was light, it was comfortable, it was the home of a stranger. The only familiar thing was the Italian coffee pot which she now picked up and put on the stove.

'Are you hungry, Timmy? You look a bit worn.'

'Not yet. Let's talk first. Why did you not come to see me Ma? Let's get this over.'

'I was ill,' she said, and I noticed that she was thin and looked older. 'Maybe I nearly died, I'm not sure, but I was in hospital with pleurisy and pneumonia. It was a long time before I could look for you – and during that time I found out about the whole separate life you had led with that dreadful Swan, I thought you must have turned into someone different and maybe did not want to see me anyway. Or not want me to have found out what happened. Would you *like* a visit? How did I know, I could not decide. But I did go to the borstal finally, the Governor showed me round.'

'You went round, when I was *there*?'

'But when it came to the point I didn't know if I could face you. Or for that matter, could *you* face *me*. You were in there for being mixed up in Swan's drug pushing, and maybe hoped I didn't know about it. To see me might just be embarrassing. I discussed it with the Governor. He said he would show me the sort of quarters where you lived, but in another building, so I would know how you were treated, and it would give me time to think. Then I went away. I couldn't imagine how you felt any more – you were lost to me – so I couldn't decide what to do.'

To come all the way to see me and then do an about-face on the doorstep was nonsense. It was sad and unreal. This was Swan's doing again.

'I never pushed drugs, Ma.'

'I merely thought you and I didn't fit any more.'

'Listen,' I said. 'Forget Swan. He happened, that's all. None of what you thought of me was true, except some shoplifting. I did not come here to explain that. There is another reason. I've come to fetch you, Ma, I've got you a place – you'll never guess.' I started to feel excited again.

'*Fetch* me?'

'I've been to see Gregg.'

'Good Lord . . . so long ago . . . so remote now . . .'

I told her then in detail what had happened. But all she said, quite sharply, was, 'I don't want to see Wissingley ever again.'

'You won't have to. It's been bulldozed.'

At this the sharpness gave way to a look of great sadness which crossed her face but, as I continued talking, passed. I described the rest of my visit, the new post office, how it was so different that it would not be like going back.

'If it seems to you to be a new place, that may be a good thing,' she said. 'But I could never return.'

Before I got the train I had imagined she would leap. Now that I was here, I knew it would not be quite like that, but the way she was closed, so entirely different to what I had been quite sure about, was a huge disappointment. I sat down quietly and drank my coffee.

'What will you do then, Ma,' I asked then.

'I like it here.'

'What can you like about a town, you with your need of animals, and open land, and plants . . .'

'Concerts, friends, the things I didn't know I missed till I got them back again. They are here.'

So in some ways Wissingley had isolated her. My presence had only been one dimension – could she have been missing something all the time? But I remembered her enthusiasm, her joyful singing . . . Perhaps it was just that she had evolved and for her it would be going backwards.

'Gregg is an old rough bear, Timmy. You do see that I couldn't possibly move in? Did you really expect me to?'

Yes, I saw it now that I was here in her setting, but it had not occurred to me out on the moors where I thought we still both belonged, and felt that it would be like going home, only better, as there was a family of fellows. I tried to tell her this.

'Well you can still have your fellows, old Tim,' she said. 'I'm glad you've got a job, though I hoped you might do something better, you have a good brain.'

'In ten years I could have my own farm; it could be a house with a library and a big barn where you could organize concerts in summer . . .' But as I said this, I realized it was only a little boy's old dream, pathetic and absurd.

'Maybe you'll marry,' she said, losing interest. She had done her bit and now wished me off. 'I'm glad you caught me,' she continued. 'I'm going away for a month tomorrow and you wouldn't have found me. I'm going to Tunisia with James. I'm glad to know you're all right.'

James. None of this was remotely what I had expected.

'Why didn't you say so right away? When did you find James again – and how?'

'I ran into him by chance.'

It was typical, she had always run into people in the street or wherever she found herself – a quality I loved and that never happened to me. This was what I had always wanted for her, for us, long ago – wonderful, civilized James – yet now I felt nostalgic. Jealous perhaps, as if I was left out in the cold. I would like to go to Tunisia with James too, I had always dreamed of travelling with him.

'Good for you, Ma, I'm glad.'

'You don't look it.'

'So where's the breakfast you mentioned earlier?' I said. 'One of your special omelettes, toast that is crisp outside and still soft . . . and shall we have some more coffee?' And as she got up and became busy I continued, 'It would be quite funny if it had not all been such a mess.'

I leaned into the armchair and strained to make the unfamiliar flat seem familiar, somehow relating to her. James! I looked at the shelves trying to see the titles of the books but was suddenly too immensely weary to get up. There was a large record player, albums of music, but no piano.

I wondered then, seeing in my new focus, whether Gregg had really expected her – did he think in his limited way that she would come and simply be content to keep house? Or had he maybe sent me to clear up a mystery so I could get on with my life . . . It had seemed to me to be the proper ending. Tucked into bed in linen sheets. The last of my youth, adolescent hopes. Her thin face was shining now with the old light that came from it when she was happy, and I knew she had made her peace. Perhaps that was what I had really come to ascertain, I was the older man now, she was the child safely on her way, I was seeing us both off.

Fools expect happiness and whine when they don't have it, not seeing that it is the magician's rainbow, a transitory occurrence that will return often if undemanded. I had always followed the marsh light, the will o' the wisp, and expected a great happening – but now I knew contentment is the event, or rather, a permanent state to be earned.

She would go to Tunisia or the North Pole, into the land of James and his ideas and his care for her. I would go back to the big sky and my new friends – and the face of my old cat viewing the world from his detached seat on the dresser.